STEALING THE FIRST MATE

ELNORA ISLAND BOOK FIVE

TABITHA BOULDIN

Copyright © 2021 by Tabitha Bouldin

All rights reserved.

No part of this book may be reproduced in any form or by any electronic or mechanical means, including information storage and retrieval systems, without written permission from the author, except for the use of brief quotations in a book review.

ISBN: 978-1-951839-23-9

Celebrate Lit Publishing

304 S. Jones Blvd #754

Las Vegas, NV, 89107

http://www.celebratelitpublishing.com/

1

For every great day aboard the *Pirate's Treasure*, there were those random, pesky days capable of making Nigel "Davy" Jones want to hurl his tricorn replica hat into the ocean. After he'd stabbed it with his cutlass and burned the wool contraption to cinders, he would spread its ashes over Mimosa's salty shores. This Saturday morning walked the tightrope between joy and disaster.

Shoving those thoughts into the furthest recesses where they wouldn't frighten customers—especially the little ones—Nigel lowered his towering height to four-year-old levels by squatting on the balls of his feet. Good thing he wasn't a cowboy wearing spurs.

He worked his voice into a tender cadence. "You're certain?"

Blonde pigtails bobbed. With a sniffle, his latest reluctant swabbie—aka helper—scrubbed tears from her eyes and hiccupped. "Davy Jones is scary." Her shoulders trembled, followed by a deep sob. "I don't wanna go."

Legs trembling from the pressure of holding the same position, Nigel rocked back until he could sit on the deck and cross his legs. The deck shifted beneath them as the engines chugged, pulling them across open water. Despite the girl's insistence she wanted nothing to do with the pirate boat tour around Independence Islands, they were already aboard and on their way.

He swiped the tricorn off his head and settled it in his lap. The long, purple plume tucked into the hatband danced beneath the girl's chin. She giggled and sniffled. *How do kids do that?*

The crew shouted from behind Nigel, their signal the skit had begun. Nigel waved, indicating they should proceed without him. Captain Black would tell the tale of Reginald Merriweather as the *Treasure* sailed from Mimosa, past Merriweather, and back again. Voices chorused together in song and stomping feet beat a rhythm across the deck. The boards beneath Nigel shivered with the impact of a dozen pairs of boots.

"Can I tell you a secret?" Nigel spun the hat in a slow circle, making the feather dance.

With a nod, the young girl reached out to stroke the feather. Her parents clasped their hands together, fingers flat in prayerful repose, their eyes pleading with him to convince their baby the pirates aboard *Pirate's Treasure* would not throw her to Davy Jones' locker.

Treasure's owner, Mr. Riggins, had a NO REFUND policy that caused parental angst often enough that Nigel had an entire spiel prepared for most situations. This though. This was a first. Her insistence that *he* was THE Davy Jones had sucker-punched him. Her fear had been palpable, and his need to fix the world reared its haughty head.

"I'm not a real pirate. My name is Nigel." He held out a hand. Keeping his distance, he allowed the girl to choose whether she would shake his hand. "I'm only pretending. Like in the movies."

Tiny fingers grazed his palm as her gaze jerked up to meet his. "I'm CC."

"Pleasure to meet you, CC." He dropped the tricorn onto her

head, and she laughed when her eyes disappeared beneath the brim. "I promise you'll be safe with me...and my friends."

CC sniffed again and palmed his hat from her head. She shoved the brown wool lump onto his head and held out a hand. "Okay."

That was easy enough.

Nigel looked up at her parents, silently asking for permission. When they both nodded, Nigel stood and led them toward the group of pirates and tourists laughing and singing around the ship's mast. One couple hooked elbows and whirled around with a raucous, "We've got a tale you'll not believe. A tale of a man who walks the seas!"

A woman's voice drifted down from the crow's nest. Not just any voice. Darcy. The wind ripped her words out to sea before they could be understood, but Nigel could pick Darcy out of the cacophony without fail. He looked up in time to see Darcy swing out of the crow's nest and grasp tightly to the rope ladder. Scrambling down quicker than a monkey, she landed by his side with a thump of her black pirate boots.

CC glanced up, and nothing short of awe could explain her rapt attention. Her voice ticked upward an octave. "There are *girl* pirates?"

Nigel grinned. Apparently, the four other women dancing around the deck hadn't caught CC's attention. He couldn't say he blamed her. Darcy caused the same gape-mouthed expression for him too.

"Are you kidding? We're the best pirates." Darcy patted the replica blunderbusses strapped crossways over her hips. "No one messes with girl pirates."

Before CC could respond, a loud squawk swamped the shouting and dancing pirates. Captain Black waved his tricorn in a wide arc as his other hand spun the captain's wheel. "Bernie incoming!"

CC's eyes widened and filled with tears.

Darcy squatted, bringing herself eye level with the girl. "Aw, don't worry about ole Bernie. He'll land up there with Cap'n." She winked and pointed at the pelican, making lazy circles above the crew. "Watch. Here he goes."

Bernie tucked his wings and glided downward, spinning through the currents like a wobbly top. With another long squawk and an impressive wing flap, Bernie landed on the table to the Captain's left. He bobbed his head and waddled to the edge before reaching out his bill and butting Captain Black's shoulder.

CC's eyes threatened to pop from their sockets if she spread them any wider. "Wow. Wait'll I tell my friends I saw pirates with a pet pelican." She took her parents' hands and pulled them toward the group of kids watching Captain Black interact with Bernie.

Darcy grinned and popped upright. A regular jack-in-the-box, that one. Never could sit still for long. Drove their teachers crazy, and since they were all homeschooled together, Nigel had been privy to every moment of Darcy's immense personality.

She elbowed Nigel in the ribs and wiggled her heavily penciled eyebrows. Her pirate makeup never ceased to amuse as she always went over the top with heavy eyeliner and super thick eyebrows. Her lips were scarlet today, something he'd been trying to avoid noticing since she stepped aboard just before sunrise.

Nigel nudged her back and cackled when she pursed her lips in a pout. Her straight, black hair teased her cheeks as the wind whipped over the bow. He liked her curls better. The days she let the natural curls spring around her face in long ringlets, he ached to twist one around his fingers. Darcy thought the curls made her look too much like her ancestor, the infamous pirate Anne Bonny. She despised the legacy Bonny'd left behind and always looked for a way to separate herself from her history.

Hard to do when her dad operated a pirate boat tour that regaled tourists with pirate legends.

Nigel's fake dreads scratched against his neck, a familiar sensation after so many years aboard ship. The silence caressed his soul with a lover's touch. Too bad he could never tell Darcy how much he loved every piece of her past and her present. Or how much he longed to become part of her future. She'd become his treasure so long ago there wasn't a time in his memory when he'd not been in love with her.

"I'm always surprised how good you are with the kids." Darcy stuck her thumbs in her leather belt and rocked back on her heels.

"You shouldn't be. I love kids. They're the reason I'm out here sweating to death in a made-up pirate costume." Nigel mimicked her stance, his cutlass hilts bumping against his wrists and bringing him fully back to where they stood and the woman he could never have. "You should go out with us more. Most of this new crew doesn't even know who you are."

Darcy's gaze jumped to meet his, her blue eyes narrowing to slits. "And I don't want them to know. I don't want special treatment because Dad owns the *Treasure*."

"Best not let them see you slacking then." Nigel darted into the swarm of pirates dancing around the deck. Jerking his blunted cutlass from his waist, he punched it into the air, hooked elbows with one of the crew and joined in the ruckus of shouts and cheers.

Overhead, the bell clanged a warning. Bernie added a squawk to the clamor as pirates scrambled across the deck. Their tour came to an end, as Mimosa's dock drifted into sight. Captain Black nodded to Nigel, and he moved toward the cannon on the starboard deck. With a quick motion, he ignited the gunpowder and sent a deck-shuddering boom across the empty ocean. Cheers erupted from the crew and their guests. Even CC jumped up and down and waved in wild circles.

Captain Black steered them with an expert hand, and they bumped against the dock with barely a jostle. One of the new crew members settled the gangplank, then another strung up the rope for passengers to grasp as they made their way down the solid walkway.

Nigel scanned the docks, keeping track of guests as they left the *Treasure* and returned to Mimosa, where they could find almost anything a vacationer could ask for. A flash of white and gray, accompanied by an undeniably familiar bark, pulled him from the deck and toward Mel, his friendly dog groomer, who held his canine's leash with a firm grip.

Darcy ran past him and fell to her knees in front of Shep, Nigel's Old English Sheepdog. Her arms wrapped around Shep, who woofed and tried to slobber his way through the layers of makeup. Darcy laughed and leaned away from the doggy advances.

Nigel staggered to a stop as every muscle tightened with desire.

Mel passed the leash over to Darcy and stalked toward Nigel. She halted less than a foot away and lowered her sunglasses, unleashing a full glare.

"Come on, Mel. Don't give me that look. It was an emergency."

"Picking up your dog on Elnora, grooming him, and spending hours on the ferry to bring him to you on Mimosa is not an emergency." Mel crossed her arms and practically sizzled with each word.

Nigel offered his sincerest puppy dog face.

Before he could get a word out, Mel sliced through the air with her hand. "No. Don't give me that look. I'm mad at you." Her voice cracked on the last word as a grin wiggled loose. Shep barked again, drawing Mel's attention.

Nigel pitched his voice low enough so Darcy wouldn't hear. "Mr. Riggins is threatening eviction if Shep doesn't stop barking and digging holes under the fence." His hands worried the sash around his waist, twisting the red cotton into a knot. "I couldn't leave him home alone."

"This is ridiculous, Nigel. You should tell Darcy what's going on. Surely, she can help you. It's her own father making your life miserable. What I can't understand is why?"

A crowd of people converged around them, the next group of passengers amassing at the gangplank. An elderly man bumped Darcy, almost knocking her to the ground. Nigel elbowed his way through the crowd before Mel could press her interrogation. Telling Darcy her father wanted Nigel out of her life was out of the question. Darcy would demand to know why, much as Mel had. More. Darcy would not let well enough alone. She'd been his best friend since they met in first grade. Her sense of justice would drive her to investigate. Nigel could never let her learn the truth.

2

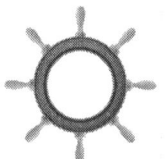

Darcy swung her leg from side to side, the motion offsetting her need to jump up and run away from yet another disastrous date. After leaving work on the *Treasure*, she'd raced home to her little cottage on Elnora Island to shower, change into her new dress, and race back to Mimosa.

Why had she ever imagined this would work out? Today's failure of choice, Carl, sat across the tiny table and waved his arms wildly as he emphasized the epic tale of his heroism. That, she could handle. But the broccoli floret sticking out between his front teeth threatened to capsize their floundering dinner date.

She'd tried to point out the bit of greenery poking its head from between a set of perfectly straight, too-white teeth. Carl hadn't listened, choosing instead to regale her with a story of apparent wit. Since he laughed loud enough to have people in every nook and cranny risking cricks as they rubbernecked in his direction, Darcy could only presume he found himself hilarious.

With her elbow propped on the table—something her mother would have frowned upon—Darcy let her chin drop into her palm. Soft music pumped out from speakers hidden somewhere overhead. Silverware clinked amidst a hum of conversation. Behind her, a loud cackle shot through the air. Darcy jumped, banging her knee on the chair tucked in beside her. Carl had tried for a booth, but Darcy begged for a table. Claiming claustrophobia prevented her from becoming trapped out of sight. Her line of disastrous dates had led her here, to the subterfuge of hiding friends in case she needed a rescue.

Her leg jigged faster, the red heel blurring until it flew off with a whoosh. Light from crystal chandeliers glittered across the glossy red surface. Darcy kept her gaze locked, her eyes widening as the red missile clanked, bounced twice, then settled beneath the white tablecloth of the couple two tables over. Candlelight flickered from their tucked-in booth, and they leaned away from each other.

Carl continued to prattle. She had to commend his focus. Talk at the other table stuttered to a halt. All around them, little gasps echoed, followed by hands lifted to cover shocked mouths. Darcy pulled her face into an apologetic smile and lifted her hand in a tiny wave. The woman who had nearly been nailed by Darcy's shoe gave Carl a single glance before her face melted into an expression of understanding. She reached over and patted the man's hand. Carl would never suspect Darcy of sabotage. Mel and Zeke looked as piqued as the other customers.

Darcy's breath whooshed out when Mel stood. The little black dress Darcy had talked Mel into buying the month before hugged her every curve. She risked a glance at Zeke, Mel's date. Oh, yes. Those hours spent with Mel bemoaning the needlessness of this particular dress had paid off. For a moment, she regretted signaling Mel. If Zeke's narrow-eyed expression was any indication, he regretted the interruption even more. The tense lines evaporated when Mel tucked her arm around his and pressed a kiss to his cheek.

Sigh. Darcy released a heavy breath. *Any day, Lord. Sorry to be a nuisance, but could You send my prince charming soon?*

Zeke nudged Darcy's shoe with his foot and jerked his head toward the door. Mel swooped up the shoe and darted forward. "Darcy! There you are. I've been looking *everywhere* for you." With her hand around Darcy's arm, Mel hauled Darcy to her feet the instant her foot slid into the heel and propelled her toward the door.

Zeke dropped money near Darcy's plate of roasted chicken with snow peas, placed his hand on his chest with an expression of profound apology, and backed away.

A waiter paused mid-stride to watch their escape. He lifted the platter of food into the air, sending the tang of lemon pepper chicken to cover the yeasty aroma of fresh garlic bread. The room froze, glasses half raised to waiting lips as though a movie had been paused.

Carl appeared stupefied. He deflated faster than a balloon with a fist-sized hole. Darcy could almost hear the hiss as his pompous hot air leaked out with a whoosh. He dropped his hands onto the table, palms flat against the surface. All the bravado wilted, but he reached for his fork and began shoveling food into his mouth faster than a goldfish eating food flakes.

Mel continued pulling on Darcy's arm all the way down the sidewalk and around the corner. Once out of sight, she stopped and glanced over her shoulder. Her laughter bubbled and bounced out when Zeke tugged his navy-blue suit jacket together and worked the button through the hole. "You can take the boy out of the corporation, but you can't take the schmoozing out of the boy."

"What's that supposed to mean?" Zeke ran both hands through his hair, messing up his styled curls. Several cars zoomed by, sending the stench of exhaust and garbage to overpower Monsel's garlic and yeast aroma that had followed Zeke out the door.

Mel waved her hand toward the restaurant. "You apologized as though you'd mortally offended him." She snorted a laugh. "For a minute, I thought you might sit down and have dinner in Darcy's place."

"I can't help it if I'm polite." Zeke draped his arm across Mel's shoulders and motioned toward the ferry. "Where you headed, Darcy?"

"Home." Darcy followed the enigmatic couple down Mimosa's busy streets. Their tourist trap island kept people busy and away from the five Independence Islands they called home. Hopper for Mel. Merriweather for Zeke. Elnora for Darcy. She bit back a sigh when Zeke ran his hand up and down Mel's bare arm. *Smitten. Twitter-pated.* Oh, how she loved Disney's version of love. Whatever trite word came to mind, it fit Mel and Zeke like a second skin. When would it be her turn to find true love? She shivered with anticipation of her glorious moment. For her, falling in love would be akin to skydiving. That moment of *knowing* as she left the plane and leaped out on faith. That's what love would be for her.

To be denied that...again... It more than annoyed her. It infuriated. There was no justice if someone who wanted love so desperately couldn't find it after searching for so many years.

"I think I'll never get married. I'll just live like Paul."

"Paul the garbage man?" Zeke sent a confused look in her direction. "I thought he was married."

"Paul the Apostle, you loon." Darcy flung her hair over her shoulder and reached for her ferry ticket. "Paul thought it was better if men never married. The same can be said for women too."

"I'm not sure that's exactly what Paul meant. If you feel that's where God is truly leading you, I won't argue." Mel popped her sunglasses into place and twisted her hair into a low bun. After securing the curly mass with a hairband, she waved toward the restaurant. "Sometimes I think you're being overly critical."

Darcy opened her mouth to argue, then snapped it shut. She had expectations. But was it too much to ask for a guy to have a little class? Or to hold her purse? Couldn't a real man care enough to stop talking now and then? "Even you have to admit he wasn't for me."

"Okay, yes. Maybe. But, Darcy, he was trying so hard to impress you. Can you fault him for that? You're like a package of dynamite. You intimidate people. Whether you mean to or not."

Darcy's eyebrows scrunched together, and she lifted her hands in an I-can't-help-it pose. "I'm not asking for a superhero. Just a nice, normal guy who loves me for me. And don't throw Nigel in my face. We're friends. We'll always be friends. Nothing more." Her vehemence surprised her.

Mel's eyebrows shot up, even as she smiled. Zeke had stepped a few paces away, presumably to give them a chance to chat. Mel pointed her ticket in Darcy's face, the paper sending out a sliver of breeze and the hint of Mel's fruity perfume. "I had no intention of bringing up Nigel, but since you did, you could do a lot worse than Nigel Jones."

"I could do a lot better too." The words shot out before she could think about, or stop them. And as soon as they left her mouth, regret roared up. Darcy pressed her palms to her temples and shook her head. "I didn't mean that. Not the way it sounded. I love Nigel, *as a friend*. I can't imagine spending the rest of my life with him. It'd be too weird. Can you imagine waking up to your best friend's face every morning?" Despite her words, a peculiar flutter woke in her stomach.

"Yeah, I can." Mel's eyes softened, and she looked over at Zeke. "I can't imagine waking up next to anyone else." She twisted her fingers together and shook her head. "Why on earth did I let you talk me into this dress? There aren't any pockets."

"Stop fretting." Darcy nudged Mel toward Zeke. "You've got

Zeke drooling over you. Not having pockets is worth the look on his face right now."

Zeke hadn't taken his eyes off Mel the entire afternoon. Every time Darcy glanced over during dinner, Zeke stared at Mel like he'd won the races. His mooning made her want to sigh and cry at the same time. *Dumb romantic pirate genes.* Darcy groused and crossed her arms.

Mel watched Zeke, her lips tilting up in a goofy smile.

Darcy gave her a push. "Oh, go on already. You're as bad as he is." In fact, she was surprised Zeke hadn't asked the big question yet. Even though he and Mel had only been dating for six months, he was over the moon in love.

She wanted that with a fierceness that would shock most people. The perfect man was out there somewhere. She'd find him if she had to turn over every rock across the Islands. *You deserve perfection, Darcy.* Her dad's words surfaced and refused to be quieted. He would never accept Nigel as a son-in-law. *Only the best for my baby girl. It's one thing to own a fleet of ships, it's another to desire nothing more than to amuse children.* Darcy snorted as she boarded the ferry, drawing surprised looks from a few touristy-looking passengers. *What does that even mean? God, please help me understand.*

3

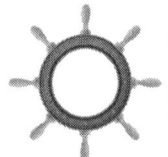

Silhouetted in moonlight, Darcy's shadow hugged the sand. The thoughtful tilt of her chin tugged at Nigel's already eviscerated heart. *When, Lord? When will You take these feelings away? I can't love her. She deserves better. After what I've done, I deserve this pain, but I wish You would take it away.*

When she reached up and grasped a strand of hair to twirl around her fingers, Nigel stepped into view. "You'll go bald if you keep that up."

Her hands dropped, a guilty dart of her eyes showing she either regretted the motion or regretted getting caught. Knowing Darcy like he did, most likely the latter.

"What're you doing out here?" Her voice carried a twinge of sadness. The ice cream and the knockout red dress finished the final clue. Another bad date.

Nigel lowered himself to the sand and swung his legs out. Across the Islands, angry surf pounded against the rocks. Here on Elnora, it washed across smooth sand with a gentle lullaby. No caves waited to be filled with water as the tide surged and crashed. Their flat island was perfect for growing grapes for the local wineries, not so much for deep-sea spelunking. He grinned at the brief memory of his last diving adventure with Darcy. They'd found an amazing coral reef. He should offer to take her out again.

Branches crackled and rubbed together with a puff of breeze that fluttered Darcy's hair. Before he could offer his heart up again for sacrifice, he forced the idea of him and Darcy back into the box where it belonged. "Saw your car when I took Shep out for a run. Thought I'd see how the date went."

Darcy waved the ice cream under his nose. "Does this answer your question?"

He looked inside, noted only dregs of melted ice cream remained, and nodded. "Want to talk about it?"

"What's wrong with me?"

That went downhill fast. Pain crimped his insides at her quiet question. Darcy wasn't one to express solemn, heartfelt desires to him. She preferred the steamroller approach. Find a target and charge full steam ahead, regardless of obstacles. Her normal attitude ranked somewhere in the realm of cotton candy, rainbows, and unicorns. Obnoxiously optimistic, it took serious worry to drag Darcy Riggins down to the mortal plane.

"We've been friends a long time, Darcy." Nigel rubbed his beard and stumbled to a halt.

Darcy spun the spoon in a slow whirl and eyed him. "Just say it. You've always told me the truth. I can handle it."

If only that were true. Nigel locked his right hand in a vise grip over his left wrist, stopping the offending member trying to edge closer to Darcy. Her father's words beat a samba inside his brain. Darcy was off limits. No matter this was the twenty-first century. Mr. Riggins owned Nigel. With enough dirt and old secrets to sink a tanker, Darcy's father had made it clear Nigel could be her friend, but anything else would not be tolerated. One wrong move and even friendship would be off the table.

"There's nothing wrong with you."

Darcy scoffed, throwing her head back and emitting a sound

so cynical Nigel had to face her just to make sure she wasn't choking.

"If that's true, why can't I find someone who wants to marry me?" Her head stayed tilted, her gaze on the stars twinkling overhead. "Wait. Let me rephrase that. I could marry anyone, but I do have a few standards. Why can't I find *that* man?" Subtle moonlight bathed her face as its fullness lifted over the horizon and spread across the mirror flatness of the ocean. "I know it's a silly dream, but is it wrong to want to be married? Everyone keeps telling me I have time. I'm not that old. Why rush?" Crumpling the ice cream carton into a ball, she blew out a harsh breath. "It's not wrong to want to be a wife and a mother."

"I guess it won't do me any good to remind you that you might be trying too hard?" His hand twitched toward her arm. He craved a moment of contact. Just one to carry him over. The selfishness of his desire forced his hand back. He was supposed to be here for Darcy. Not himself. *Remember what happened last time you wanted someone as much as you want Darcy. No. That's not true. Never wanted anyone as much as I want her.* His shoulders slumped forward, and he gripped his hands tighter, even pulled them against his stomach to prevent any errant touch.

Darcy's silence stretched too long.

Never one to remove herself from conversation, the change intrigued him. Turning only his face, Nigel caught her staring directly at him. He froze, afraid to even breathe as Darcy reached her hand toward him. Pinching her thumb and forefinger together, she pulled a rogue string from his shoulder. His breath left in a rush, and his eyes narrowed when she smiled. He sounded like a schoolgirl with a crush.

A hint of concern pinched her lips and shadowed her eyes, but the smile promised her melancholy wouldn't last. She scooted closer and lowered her head to his shoulder. "At least I'll always have you for a friend. We can grow old and grumpy together."

The fact she assumed he would never marry pricked his anger. Who was he kidding? There was no one else for him. Not now. Not ever, unless God stepped in. Darcy had no idea. And she never would. His unjustified anger cooled as he released a breath. None of this was her fault. "Yeah, maybe they'll ask us to reboot *Grumpy Old Men* and make it The Grumpy Old Friends." The weight of her head on his shoulder should have brought solace instead of regret. "What was wrong with this one?"

Her wispy sigh made his heart melt like buttercream in July.

"According to Mel, nothing."

"And you say?" He refused to move even a centimeter for fear she'd lift her head. A curl brushed her cheek and for a brief flash of insanity, he wished he had the right to take the strand between his fingers. Her jasmine perfume settled around him, wrapping him in memories of racing down the beach with her by his side. What a young, foolish kid he'd been to think he could ever deserve someone like her.

"I don't want to talk about it anymore. Any excitement on the *Treasure* after I left?" Darcy tucked the curl behind her ear, and he could hear the smile in her voice. "Scare any more kids?"

When she curled her hands around his arm and bumped against his side, he knew what heaven must feel like. "Ogre that I am, I had a dozen run away screaming between your leaving and closing time."

A laugh burst out, and he grinned. Oh, to hear that sound every day.

Beyond them, a couple walked the beach, hand in hand. Darcy sighed the dreamy sigh of a romantic heart and squeezed his arm.

"Come on." Nigel stood, pulling Darcy as he rose. "Enough sulking."

"What? Where are we going? I'm not sulking." She said the words, but her lower lip pouted in a generous curve that shot straight to his gut.

Clamping her arm against his side, he pulled her toward the water. "Swimming."

She balked, just as he'd known she would. "I can't swim in this." While one hand rested on her cocked hip, the other clamped firmly around his arm. A devious grin spread out over her face, and she peeked toward the row of houses lining the beach. "You're trying to trick me again. Like the time you told me there were leeches in the marsh because you were afraid."

"No," he shot back. "I was terrified." He waited for her grin. "You wanted to hunt for wild horses. I know you, Darcy Riggins. I would have ended up getting a spanking that would have left my backside sore for weeks."

Her hand lowered, and he tugged her again. "No swimming. Got it. You can still walk on the beach, can't you? Or is that dress too fancy for walking?" He gave it a long look, using the excuse to its full advantage. All the moisture fled his mouth at the luscious curves the red material made no attempt to hide. He knew nothing about fashion…or dresses. But her bare arms glowing in the moonlight as a flush spread across her cheeks? Oh, yeah. He liked that. Frowning, he shrugged at her. "I suppose it's a nice dress though."

Her angry splutter spurred him on, and soon she was chasing him across the sand. Barefoot, her red heels dangled from one hand while the other jabbed in his direction. Her red hem dragging in the sand caught her attention, and Darcy stopped long enough to gather a handful of skirt before taking off running again.

He laughed and ran knee-deep into the ocean, out of reach. Darcy never slowed. Instead, she gave a squeal and jumped straight toward him, landing flush against his chest at the same moment a wave crashed against the backs of his thighs. Off balance, he wobbled. Darcy shrieked and threw her arms around his neck as they went down.

Ocean water closed over his head, but he barely felt the

waves. Everything he ever wanted, he held in his arms. God help him, he never wanted to let her go.

Too soon, they surfaced. Darcy brushed her flattened hair away from her face and laughed. "Got you."

"Not for long." His heart jackknifed as he pulled them from the water then released her. "You should go inside. It's late, and I'd hate for you to ruin your dress."

Her face clouded as she tugged the soaked material away from her legs. "We should do this again sometime. Maybe take Shep for a swim."

"Sure. I'm pretty busy with work next week, but we'll catch up sometime."

4

After church Sunday on Elnora, and traveling across Merriweather with Mel on Monday, Tuesday began at Mimosa's only riding stable. Darcy swung the saddle over the back of a brown and white spotted gelding, grunting with the effort.

Her ride for the day turned to look at her, his warm brown eyes calm and serene. "Nothing bothers you, does it, Patches?" She patted the white neck before reaching for the cinch. After tugging everything into place, she grabbed Patches' reins and led him to the line of waiting horses. He nudged her shoulder with his nose and whuffled her shoulder with his lip, knocking her hat to the side with his cheek. "Stop that." Darcy righted her hat and stopped long enough to scratch the whorl on Patches' forehead.

"Problem, Darcy?" Melbourne's voice crackled with his smoker's cough before regaining a vestige of vigor. "Got a group ready to head out. Waiting on you."

Another pat. Patches nudged her chest, leaving behind a streak of white hair on her gray t-shirt. "No problem. On my way there now." Putting her left foot in the stirrup, Darcy swung into the saddle and toed her boot into the right stirrup. Patches bobbed his head. He loved the trails, and his joy worked through each muscle, edging up into Darcy's legs with his in-place jog.

Melbourne pushed his hat back with one thumb and gave Patches' shoulder a hearty pat. Sunlight beamed over his tough-as-leather skin, deepening the lines that fanned out from his eyes and mouth. "Might have trouble with the big guy on Champ. Thinks himself a cowboy. Got the boots to prove it." A gleam sparkled in his eyes, and the lines creased together with his smile.

Barely resisting the urge to snort like one of the horses, Darcy glanced toward the group of ten waiting for her to lead them out on the trail. She spotted him right away. Brand-new boots glistened, reflecting like mirrors. Even better, the ten-gallon hat perched on his riot of curls pressed down on his ears until they stuck straight out. He waved his arm at the group and rocked back in the saddle. Champ shifted to compensate, and the man lurched forward, nearly unseated by the simple movement. He fell on Champ's neck, and the gelding turned toward Darcy with an expression that could only be pleading.

She muffled a laugh behind her hand and gave Patches the signal to walk by squeezing with her thighs. Patches blew out a snort and shuffled forward in a steady plod. The group had already been given the rundown on how the rides operated, and they were expected to fall in line behind her once she passed the corral gate. From there, they would travel the three-mile loop through the pines toward the beach, ride through the surf for a half-mile, then return. Before she even made it to the trees, Mr. Cowboy tried to urge Champ faster. His "hiya" and the sound of his heels thumping the horse's sides sent Darcy's temper straight from simmer to boiling eruption.

Tugging the reins, she turned Patches around. At the sight of her scowling face, the riders between her and the troublemaker raised their eyebrows and shifted in their saddles. Darcy called out a "whoa," halting every horse in the line. Trained by Melbourne to listen to voice commands, Darcy had spent weeks with the elderly man and each horse so they would listen to her above any instruction given to them by their riders.

Cowboy continued his thumping, his legs coming out wide and hitting with enough force to make Champ flinch but refuse to obey. "Mr. Harris, stop this nonsense immediately." His name popped into her head from the list she'd scanned moments before saddling Patches. "You know the rules of this ride. We walk our horses. Champ knows he's not supposed to move in front of anyone. It doesn't matter how much you suggest he do otherwise, he won't disobey his training."

Harris scowled, ripped the hat from his head, then smacked Champ on the rump with the oversized headwear. "Get up, you lazy bag of bones!"

Darcy moved Patches to Champ's side, and the two friends began chuffing at each other in their own conversation. "I'll not warn you again. If you lay one more finger on that horse, I'll call the police."

Melbourne made his way across the brittle grass, cell phone in hand. His boots thumped, a slight limp becoming apparent with each stomp. "Mr. Harris, you are no longer welcome on this ride, nor are you welcome at my establishment. I suggest you dismount immediately. I'll be happy to refund your money since you're unable to make it onto the trail." Worry lined Melbourne's forehead and tightened his eyebrows.

Darcy reached for Champ's reins, but Mr. Harris yanked them to the side, pulling Champ's head around. The horse squealed at the sudden movement and shifted his hooves. Darcy reached over, grabbed the headstall behind Champ's ears and pulled down. The slick, black leather slid over Champ's ears, past his eyes, and when Champ released the bit, away from his head, leaving Mr. Harris with a tangle of useless leather.

Still raging, he lifted his legs to kick again. Darcy nudged Patches closer, pressing the man's leg hard between the two warm bodies. His other leg would be pressed tight against the fence. "Don't." Her voice growled, low and threatening. A tone she almost never had to use. One that would shock Mel and Nigel if they ever heard. Working here at Switchback Ranch had added a layer of steel to the bubbly personality she knew grated on more than a few nerves.

Pinned on both sides, sweat began to pool and trickle down the man's face. Good. Darcy had no sympathy for him. Anyone who would try to abuse their privilege—especially after already being warned of the rules—deserved a little squeeze.

When he winced and lowered his hands, Darcy let Patches ease up an inch.

The sight of a police car rolling to a stop in the parking lot brought a rush of relief to Darcy's lungs. Melbourne hadn't waited on her to decide the call was necessary. He loved his horses too much to let anyone hurt them. If he had to cancel the ride and lose out on a day's worth of money to keep his horses safe, he would. Hands shaking, Melbourne waited at the corner of the bright red barn and left Darcy to keep the man in check. Fine. She could handle this.

Lieutenant Johnson stepped from the car and weaved around the vehicles before he reached the flat stretch of land between him and the riders. The tall and broad lieutenant covered the distance in long strides, never taking his eyes off the ruckus. Sarge, Lieutenant Johnson's K-9 shepherd stood at attention on the backseat. His head jerked back in a bark, but the sound was lost between the glass and distance.

Sweat trickled down Darcy's back, and a fine sheen covered

the riders' faces. A dark patch spread out across Champ's palomino coat. No doubt a mixture of heat and nerves. His hooves danced in place. Patches whickered and leaned against his friend. The remaining nine riders shuffled, fidgeted with the reins, and cast the occasional glance full of annoyance. Leather creaked when a woman leaned forward to comb her fingers through her mount's mane. Sugar and Sprinkles chomped their bits, jingling the metal, while a raven circled overhead and cawed.

"What seems to be the problem?" His voice, pitched deep in an intimidating gravel, rumbled down Darcy's spine. Legs braced in a wide stance and hands on hips, Johnson cocked his head toward Melbourne.

"These people," Cowboy spat, "won't let me ride. What sort of place offers trail rides then won't let people actually *ride?*"

Johnson stepped forward, motioned for Darcy to back up, and placed his hand on the saddle's pommel once the way cleared. "Why don't you come down from there and we'll talk this out. Let these nice people get on with their ride. I'm sure we can find a solution that suits everyone."

Melbourne made his way to the group and patted Champ's shoulder. The gelding turned his head toward his owner and lipped his pocket in search of a treat. Pulling out a carrot, Melbourne removed the reins from Mr. Harris's hands, moved them into a loop around Champ's neck, and gave a tug. Champ stepped from the line and followed Melbourne like a puppy.

Darcy swallowed her anger, loosened her muscles, then asked Patches to move back to the front again. All around, the riders heaved sighs of relief. Horses mouthed their bits. A few shook their heads, sending manes dancing in the wind. The scent of warm horseflesh and leather calmed the last tight muscle across her spine. "Okay, everyone, follow me." Darcy listened for the clomp of hooves that would signal the horses moving into place behind her. They started slow, letting the riders settle before the rhythm increased as all nine moved forward.

Tempers flared in the background with raised voices, followed by Sarge's bark and a menacing growl. *So, Johnson thinks something's going on with Mr. Harris. Makes sense.*

Each step into the thin thread of trees brought an extra blip of joy. Conversations began, slow like the horses' plodding hooves, before they eased into a steady beat. Mothers chatted about kids. Husbands asked about the most recent ballgame. Darcy bit off a sigh and enjoyed a smile. Even on vacation and when doing something away from the kids, this group couldn't stop talking about typical family dinner-table topics.

Someone called her name, the sharpness of the tone indicating this wasn't the first time they'd tried to get her attention. Shaking off her thoughts, Darcy turned her head toward the group. She couldn't afford to lose her concentration out here. The horses she could trust. The people, not so much.

"How long till we get to the beach?" A chorus of voices echoed the question. Smiles rose across every face when Darcy assured them only a few minutes separated them from beachy shoreline and a trip through ocean waves. Something about riding horses through the surf seemed to be one of those dreams people had. Darcy could understand it to a point, but since she rode horses down the beach four or five times a week, the gusto she always saw from visitors had waned in herself.

Patches took the step from wooded trail to the sandy beach, and Darcy's shoulders lifted. Her head tilted toward the sun as if she was a sunflower looking for light. At least there would be no proposals today. Thank God for small miracles. She couldn't tolerate witnessing another proposal on horseback while riding through the surf. It was romantic, and it made for lovely memories, but she'd seen too many in the past few years for it to make an impact anymore. All it did was break her heart a little more each time.

Nigel floated through her thoughts, eliciting a smile. The intensity of his gaze and the way he threw himself heart and soul into his work were part of what made him so popular on the *Treasure*. He would be proud of her for taking action today.

5

He'd made it a week without seeing Darcy. Like a drowning man starved for oxygen, he craved her presence. To see her smile or hear her laugh. Nigel's feet pounded across the sand with the rhythm of a man desperate to escape. Shep bounded alongside, his tongue flapping with every leap. Waves threatened to wash over his feet with every stride, but he refused to run in the soft sand above the tideline. They would have to stop soon, but the dock beckoned. Nigel pressed on, sweat already tracking down his spine and dripping from his beard even though the sun barely hung above the horizon.

Summer bore down on them, bringing all the fun of vacation to mix with the atmosphere of never having to leave your favorite place. Captain's Day rested around the corner, the all-important shindig of the year as far as the islanders were concerned. Yesterday, he'd seen a parade of people gathering supplies, a sure sign their anticipation had only begun.

Shep cut in front of Nigel, almost sending him to the ground. The leash jerked in his hand, spinning him to a halt as the excited canine turned back the way they'd come. "It's not time for your grooming yet. I won't let you miss Mel." He scratched Shep's curly head before following the dog's line of sight.

Bernie. Flying low over the ocean, the *Treasure*'s mascot zoomed toward land. Straight at them. Lowering his front end toward the ground, Shep gave a bark and wagged his stub of a tail. Bernie answered with a squawk and wheeled around in a slow arc. "Are you two serious? We're supposed to be running. Not playing with Bernie."

Mel's truck rumbled down the nearby road, fresh off the bridge and ready to start her day on Elnora, no doubt. Grooming all the pets on the surrounding islands kept her hopping, and her snazzy new truck was where Nigel would be leaving his own dog in a couple hours. She rolled to a stop and waved. "Need a hand?"

Nigel waved her on. "We're good. I know you have a busy day ahead. See you later, though."

A second face popped up beside Mel's. Darcy. She didn't often work with Mel on Elnora since most of her time was spent at the ranch doing riding tours. Great. Nigel ran a hand through his hair, and it came back soaked and dripping with sweat. Double great. Thank goodness she couldn't smell him from there. She'd never let him live that down. Nigel waved, praying Mel would keep going and let him agonize in peace.

When she rolled forward, he turned his attention back to the unlikely duo beside him. Bernie had tucked his feet beneath him and sat on the sand. Shep stretched out on his belly, nose on his paws, inches away from the white waterfowl. "You two are hopeless." He tugged on Shep's leash. "Back to our workout."

His dog whined and poked the pelican with his nose. Nigel persisted, giving an order in a tone he expected to be obeyed. Bernie would follow, or he would wait for them to double back. Either way, Nigel needed the exercise now more than ever. He jogged toward the pier with Shep at his heels. Jutting out over the water, the pier claimed Elnora as her own. Every morning,

Nigel ran the three miles from his cottage to the pier and back. The endorphin rush energized his day and kept him from feeling trapped when he had to stay on board the *Treasure* all day.

The last half mile, he pumped his legs to their full speed, sending shooting pain through his lungs. It would be worth it when he reached the pier's shade. Sliding to a halt between two pillars, Nigel dropped his hands to his knees and sucked deep breaths until the trembling in his legs stopped.

Facing their return journey, Nigel grinned at the sight of their prints etched in moist sand. A pelican-shaped shadow wheeled overhead. Nigel took one last relaxed breath before he straightened. "Come on. Let's go home. You too, Bernie." He pointed toward his cottage. "Go." The pelican had become a regular visitor over the years after claiming the Riggins' ship as home. Shep launched forward while Bernie shot straight as an arrow toward the only blue cottage dotting the beach. All Nigel could do was shake his head and follow at a steady jog.

Half an hour later, after a shower and a breakfast of stale cereal, he shoved his feet into clean ankle socks and grabbed his cell as it chimed Darcy's ringtone. Before he could speak, Darcy bowled him over. "Kendall called. She's at the ranch with Patches. I need to go…and since it's your day off—" She hiccupped and sniffed.

Mel's voice trailed over the background noise. "Nigel, can you drive Darcy to the ranch? She can't drive like this. I can take her if you're busy."

"Where are you now?" Nigel reached for a leash. Already waiting for him beside the door, Shep whined and bumped his nose against Nigel's leg. Wrangling Shep out the door and into the truck while making plans to meet up with Mel and Darcy gave him a chance to steel his heart against the upcoming turmoil. Darcy, together with an animal in pain—an animal she loved with every atom of her existence—guaranteed a bout of waterworks to rival Alice when she first arrived in Wonderland.

And if anything could reach the chains around his heart, Darcy's tears would.

Nigel worked his way inland. Elnora's heart beat from the center of town with her tiny shops and unforgettable people. The short drive between his house and the condo where Darcy waited took Nigel down a winding dirt road. He cranked up the air and punched buttons on the radio until a familiar tune filled the air. Shep woofed and slobbered the window until Nigel pulled him away.

Darcy met his vehicle and yanked at the door almost before he stopped moving. Shep put both front paws on her shoulders, nearly pushing her over with his enthusiasm. "Is he going with us?"

"I'll take him." Mel reached for Shep, wrapped the leash around her wrist twice, and smooched to get the dog out of the truck. "You can pick him up on your way home. Or I'll drop him off tomorrow."

"Thanks, Mel." Nigel shifted into reverse after Mel closed Darcy's door and backed away. He threw up a salute, and Mel returned the gesture before heading back to her truck.

Silence between him and Darcy had never been heavy or uncomfortable. The same proved true now as she curled into the seat and pressed her fingertips to her lips. He passed her a clean, bright yellow bandana from the rearview mirror. She wiped her face with a muffled "Thanks" before her head bumped the window and she released a wobbly smile.

Nigel kept his lips sealed and allowed Darcy the time she needed to process while they headed toward the stables.

Pulling into the ranch yard with Darcy sniffing in the passenger seat, Nigel gave his mental and emotional armor a heavy tug, wrapping everything in extra layers to protect himself from the angst rolling off Darcy in waves.

She leapt from the vehicle and bolted toward the barn, leaving him to trail behind. Shoving his hands deep into the pockets of his cargo shorts, he meandered in her wake while kicking up puffs of dust with his tennis shoes. Horses whinnied from the surrounding fields. Hooves pounded dirt as a small group ran up the hill to join their herd. A young colt shoved his head into the water trough and began slinging his head from side to side. Water cascaded from the metal tub, sloshing over the colt's front legs and sending him wheeling away with a high-pitched whinny.

Nigel grinned before stepping into the barn's semi-darkness. The open-ended building allowed natural light to filter in from both sides, and overhead lighting provided enough extra to chase away the gloom. It was the heavy silence weighing against the press of sunlight that sent a prickle of unease to lift the hairs on his arms. Murmured voices from a small group clustered around a stall cast a pall over the usual hubbub and laughter. Even the horses in the surrounding stalls seemed subdued as they flicked ears toward the stall on the far right.

Darcy emerged, a black lead rope in her hand and a grunting Patches on the other end. The gelding paused and strained against the rope, pulling toward his stall. Darcy eased her hand along the rope until she could grasp the halter strap beneath Patches' chin. "Come on, big guy. You have to walk." Her voice cracked, but the firm set of her mouth showed her determination. Her tears were gone for now, a will to fight taking up residence.

Nigel hurried to take up a spot on the gelding's other side. Grasping the cheek strap, he clucked his tongue and pulled gently. Patches grunted again but lifted his front hoof and stepped forward. Kendall leaned against the stall door, her arms crossed, all her attention on the straining horse.

"What'd she say?" Nigel whispered to Darcy while they continued moving Patches up the wide aisle. The sweet scent of hay and molasses stirred with each step, mingling with horse, sweat, and leather. Nigel breathed deep and allowed the familiar scent to envelop and comfort. He should visit more often. Take a ride now and then.

Darcy's mumbled voice gave information in waves. Nigel flicked a glance in her direction. Red-rimmed eyes, bright splotches on her cheeks, and the tip of her nose was beginning to appear raw.

And the emotions were just beginning.

She touched a trembling hand to Patches' neck when the tears began. Her short hiccups and shaking shoulders shortened her stride.

Her tears ruined him, wrecked him in a way he couldn't stand because he couldn't control it. Every tear that fell cut through the iron bands around his heart, each one sizzling like acid, burning the chains and setting free that abominable organ he'd long ago cast away.

6

Taking care of a sick animal shouldn't hurt this much. Darcy patted Patches on the neck and listened to his labored breaths. With each hoof placed gingerly on the hay-strewn floor, he grunted and swayed. "Sorry, fella. You can't stop." Another pat and a swipe of her sleeve over her eyes. Tears puddled again before her hand reached her side. Blurred lines showed the encroaching stalls, forcing her to press closer to the horse's side.

Nigel stepped back when Melbourne called his name. He hesitated, hovering between turning toward the older man and staying beside her. Darcy motioned him on with a jerk of her head.

"I'll be right back."

In his absence, Darcy pressed her lips to Patches' forehead and urged him to move. Every heartbeat ached. Patches strained toward the doors, grunting when Darcy made him turn and head back down the corridor.

Muted voices mixed against the grind of horses chewing grain and bumping around their stalls. The stable should have opened hours ago. The office phone shrilled, and Patches yanked against the rope as he tried to ease his way toward the feed room.

Gary, one of Switchback's oldest hands, fielded customers at the gate. Darcy winced when a horn honked, and Gary pointed back toward the center of Mimosa. Not every customer seemed willing to accept there would be no rides today.

Nigel returned, taking his place at Patches' side. Together, they moved the gelding one step at a time. Tedious though it was, Patches' life depended on them not giving in. Nigel lifted his head when she sniffed back another wave of tears, giving her a sympathetic look over Patches' neck.

His quiet support gave her strength, but she hated the idea of breaking down like this. Of letting him see her tears. If there was one person who she could be real, raw, and vulnerable with, it was Nigel. He never made her feel like a nuisance or acted as though her sometimes crazy emotions were inconvenient. Because the bubbly personality she showed everyone wasn't the person hiding in her very center. Deep in the cavern of her heart, fear lurked in a gnawing ache, threatening to devour every good thought and bright smile.

Patches halted and turned his head toward her chest. A deep sigh fluttered his nostrils, and he lipped her shirt buttons. Darcy gently pushed his head away and clucked her tongue. "No sugar cubes for you. Not yet. Come on. Walk on." A gentle tug, another groan, and a front hoof lifted, the shoe scraping a shallow trench through the dirt. Nigel's hand wrapped around hers, adding heat to her chilled fingers as misery engulfed the barn. "We have to keep him walking. Kendall thinks he has colic. He'll recover. He just has to keep walking. She said his gut sounded horrible, but treatable since he didn't seem to have rolled while in pain and twisted his intestines."

Nigel squeezed her fingers where they overlapped beneath Patches' chin. "Then we walk."

The thought of losing the pinto gelding seared worse than a

hot iron. She couldn't fathom the idea of stepping into the barn and not seeing his gentle head stretched over the wooden half-door, bobbing in greeting. Her vision blurred again, and this time, her chin quivered as a tear slipped through. Silly to cry over an animal, perhaps, especially one who had every chance of recovering. Her heart refused the post-it she kept tacking up to cover the cracks and crevices as each step widened the pain. If this was what it felt like to possibly lose something she loved, would actual, true, human love be worth the risk?

Nigel murmured words too low for her to hear, and the lead rope tugged out of her grasp. Darcy clenched her hand, afraid to let go for fear of what releasing her hold might mean for Patches. As though he understood her pain—and maybe he did, Nigel had always felt deeply—he wrapped both arms around her and pulled her into a tight embrace.

"Kendall will walk Patches for a minute. You need a break." His arms reminded her of summers on the beach. Sand in her hair and salt on her tongue. As comfortable as Granny's peach cobbler and as familiar as biscuits straight from the oven.

"I'm fine." The wobbly dips and lifts in her voice told the lie, and Nigel only held her tighter. His strength and heat should have been oppressive here in the middle of summer, but her chilled bones accepted the warmth, reveled in it with a deep need to cling and never let go. "I shouldn't have given him that extra handful of grain." She squeezed Nigel's waist, a reflex to the guilt eating away at her insides.

"That's what's been worrying you?" Nigel's head moved, his beard brushing against her temple. The softness surprised her. When he spoke again, she leaned into the tempting movement of his jaw. "Melbourne found Patches in the grain room this morning. He'd eaten his way through half a bucket of feed. You're not at fault. Get that out of your head right now."

Nearby, a palomino whickered and was answered by the sorrel across the hall. Boots thudded and mixed with the sounds of shuffling hooves. Melbourne poured a cup of coffee, his gravelly voice complaining about the thick sludge only he dared drink. Darcy tilted her lips in a half smile. She'd continue bringing her coffee from home, thank you very much. Or, as Nigel liked to call it, her pathetic attempt at a palatable coffee house experience.

His heartbeat drummed beneath her cheek, the pulse so strong even her arms felt the steady rhythm. About the time she wanted to snuggle closer, to let him mend the bent and battered pieces of her own heart, he clasped her shoulders and pulled away. His jaw worked in a sawing motion, but only kindness radiated from his steel-gray eyes. She'd seen those eyes flash like storm clouds when confronted with injustice and melt to warm pools of molten silver in the presence of children like CC.

Nigel would be a wonderful father someday. A sudden ache tightened her throat at the image of Nigel holding a pink wrapped bundle. He needed a girl first, then a boy. Maybe a couple boys.

She choked back another flood of tear-inducing images. "Thanks. For bringing me here and staying with me."

"What are friends for?" Giving her a nod, he dropped his arms, releasing her.

Chills danced along her skin at the memory of his touch, a desperate plea for the return of his warmth.

"I'll go help Kendall." Stepping back, he kicked a metal pail, sending it crashing against a plank wall with a muffled thump. Red crept up his neck in the thin patch of visible skin between his collar and the ever-present beard.

She checked the smile forming and turned on her heel. "I'll come with you."

For the next six hours, they walked, one heavy step at a time. Every time Darcy took Patches' lead, Nigel joined her. He brought her coffee, after dumping Melbourne's hideous grime and making something palatable. Despite her lack of hunger, he brought her a sandwich and refused to leave until she'd eaten.

"I don't need a babysitter." Mouth working around the bite of turkey and cheese with fresh tomato and mustard, Darcy glowered at Nigel.

He passed her a bottle of water and unwrapped his own matching sandwich. "I bring you a sandwich and suddenly I'm a babysitter instead of a friend." He chomped a bite big enough to gag most people and leaned back against the wooden door. "Must be losing my touch."

"What I mean is, you can go home. I'm okay. Patches is going to be okay. Another hour and he'll be good as new."

"Then get ready to spend another hour with me."

"It's your day off. You should be diving, or surfing...or something."

"You really think I could enjoy myself while you're here?" He shoved the remainder of the sandwich into his mouth and washed it down before he stood again. "I wouldn't be a very good friend if I brought you here then went gallivanting off to play." Brushing his fingers through his beard, he took her trash and crumpled it in his free hand, then headed toward a trash can tucked inside the office.

How many times had he made the trip up and down the barn aisle today, never leaving her side for more than five minutes? He deserved to rest, not have his day taken up by her troubles.

An hour later, ensconced in Nigel's truck as daylight fell, Darcy let her head fall back against the headrest with a thump. "Thanks."

"For what?"

"For being here. Being my friend. Sticking with me when I get all moody and emotional. Whatever you want it to be." She shrugged and thumbed away a tear.

"Hey, now. Patches is fine. You heard Kendall. Bad case of colic, but nothing we couldn't handle. Couple days' rest and he'll be back on the trail." Nigel patted her shoulder, hesitating long enough to brush a strand of hair away from her cheek.

She managed to pull her lips into a smile. "I know. Just tired, I think." Blowing out a breath, she stretched out her legs, pointing her toes straight up, then pulling them down. "I'll be up all night worrying anyway, but at least I have plenty of homework to keep me busy."

7

Do you have time to help me study today? The text popped up on Nigel's phone late Friday night, pulling him away from the dishes he'd been trying to wash. Day-old leftovers had dried so hard, he'd been tempted to buy new plates instead of dealing with the disgusting things.

Darcy's plea for a study buddy ranked about as high in priority as a root canal, but Nigel plodded up the sandy walkway toward her sunshine yellow front door with a firm sense of anticipation cording his muscles. Not that he minded teaching, or spending time with Darcy. He'd happily walk on his hands across broken glass for the chance to spend time with her. It's what her father would say if he thought Nigel was spending too much unsupervised time with his little girl that sent a wave of panic crashing over Nigel's heart.

"You came!" Darcy flung the door open and hauled him inside, her hand fisted in his t-shirt like when they were eight years old and he'd come over for a backyard barbecue. "I thought last semester was kicking my rear, but this one is even worse. Who woulda thought linguistics would be so complicated?"

Through the beach-themed living room and straight to the pile of books covering half her powder-blue sofa, Darcy pulled Nigel over the white rug without giving him a chance to kick off his sandy sneakers or even take a deep breath of the vanilla spice air fresheners pumping fragrance from their wall-mounted homes. She pushed him down. He could have resisted the motion, but seeing this side of Darcy sent his neurons into a tailspin and eradicated his ability to contradict anything she might ask of him.

"Explain this to me." Darcy sat beside him, then reached across his lap to drag a large, green paperback into his line of sight. "I bombed my last assignment because of the whole morpheme issue. He says I'm miscounting my monomorphemes and polymorphemes. I've checked it three times and I don't understand what's wrong." She handed him a sheet of paper covered with the same sentence written out multiple times. Above each word, she'd indicated her decision of poly versus mono, then written out columns showing which words belonged in each group along with the total number of each.

Nigel scanned the chapters, then moved the book from his lap and tapped the paper, already catching on to her misunderstanding. "You're counting syllables, not morphemes. Having more than one syllable doesn't make the word a polymorpheme. Here." He retrieved a clean sheet of paper from the driftwood coffee table and scratched out the sentence. With several quick slashes and notes, he showed her the difference while offering a quick explanation. When he looked up, her eyes had glazed and rested at half-mast.

"I'm officially impressed. How do you know this? It's college level material."

"Just because I work on the ship doesn't mean I've not taken some classes." He scratched the back of his neck, praying the heat he felt there hadn't spread across his face. "I'm curious, though. If you thought I wouldn't understand it, why did you ask me to help?"

Darcy's chin dropped. She waited several beats, as though expecting him to explain or apologize for the harsh words. When he tightened his jaw, she exhaled hard enough to flutter the pages in her lap. "I missed you. And I thought this would be a good excuse to catch up. Why are you working as a pirate on a tour boat when you could be a teacher, a professor even?" Darcy snatched the paper and ran her fingers over his work. "I've spent the last three weeks scouring my textbook, talking with my professor, and cramming every article I could find on the internet, and you've just explained everything in five minutes while making it completely understandable."

"The better question is, why are you taking a linguistics class? I thought you were getting a degree in nursing."

"Changed majors." Darcy frowned at the paper, still intent on the words printed there instead of him.

Always something else between them. Nigel tried to ignore the feeling of inferiority. It wasn't Darcy's fault she didn't feel the same way. He couldn't push his emotions onto her. She would never see him as more than a friend. Even if she wanted to, her father wouldn't allow it. And Darcy loved her dad too much to hurt him by disobeying his orders. Nigel wouldn't let it come to that. He could control his love. He'd managed this long. A tight ball of agony cinched his neck. He could manage a while yet.

Shoving off from the couch, he turned his back to the sight of Darcy curled with one leg beneath her. Gray leggings covered by an oversized pink t-shirt that hit mid-thigh. Pink toenails peeked out from her bare feet, and a charm bracelet dangled from her left wrist. Hair twisted into a messy knot on top of her head with black strands escaping to frame her face. He was a goner. As Captain Jack Sparrow would say, "Nobody move! I dropped me brain." Only, he'd lost more than his brain. His heart raced at the mere idea of sitting beside her again.

He needed a distraction, and he needed it *now*.

Darcy's tiny kitchen, a mirror of his own, drew him forward. Nigel opened the freezer and stuck his head inside. The blast of freezing air cooled the heat rushing across his face but couldn't quell the rising flood heating his blood. Distraction. He needed a distraction. And fast. "What are you studying now?"

Ah! His gaze zeroed in on the pints of ice cream lining the perimeter of the freezer. Flavors he'd never heard of and curled his nose at the idea of tasting. Darcy's love of ice cream had become something of a joke between them over the years, and he'd often ask the local grocers to bring in a few crazy flavors to entice Darcy's sweet tooth.

"Criminology." Darcy shifted on the sofa, the sound of her feet sliding over the gray driftwood flooring alerting him to her movement. "You find anything you like?"

Her scent flooded into the enclosed space. How in the name of all that was holy did something so subtle and sweet sneak into the frozen depths and assault him with delicious torture? Oh, yeah. He'd found something he liked. To distract himself from the wayward thoughts, he reached for the nearest containers, pulling out two random pints and holding them out to Darcy. "Which one should I try?"

She pointed at his left hand and grinned. The glint in her eyes forced him to scan the label. Great. Just great. Pistachio ice cream. He resisted the urge to groan while handing her the carton of plain chocolate. His favorite. "Are you going to tell me what's going on or do we need to play twenty questions?" He dug two spoons from the drawer, then bumped it closed with his hip while holding out a spoon for her to take. "You were chatty enough a few minutes ago but you're as closed off now as a clam with a pearl inside."

"Nice image." Darcy ripped the top off her ice cream and

spooned a healthy bite into her mouth before she continued, covering her mouth with one hand. "Dad said get a degree. He didn't say in what. Just that I needed to have a degree." She pulled her face into a scowl and waved her spoon in imitation of Mr. Riggins. "'Progress, Darcy. We can't go backwards, receding into the piracy Anne Bonny made us famous for. We must move forward, always finding something better. We must *improve* the Riggins name, not drag it through the mud.'"

"Don't you have, like, two jobs?"

"Three."

Nigel raised his eyebrows and spooned the tiniest bite possible into his mouth. He grimaced at the flavor and shook his head while replacing the top.

Darcy grinned and held out the carton in her hand with only the one massive crater dug straight in the center. She jiggled it under his nose until he swapped cartons. "Working on the *Treasure* every other weekend, with Mel Monday and Wednesday, then at the stables with Melbourne all the other days and the remaining weekends. Except for the days I take off to work on my classes. Days like today." She shrugged one delicate shoulder. "I like all my jobs. I'm not ready to grow up and have just one job for the rest of my life."

"Who says you have to?" But he knew. Before Darcy could even utter the words, he knew. They made their way back into the living room, the ice cream doing nothing to soothe the ache burning through his chest.

"Dad says everyone should have *a* job. Not three. Only bums or weirdos work three jobs." Darcy lowered her eyes and scraped a line of green ice cream onto her spoon. "He means well. I just don't know what I want to do for the rest of my life, Nigel. I don't see myself doing the same thing every day, day after day, from now until the day I die." She huffed and flopped onto the couch.

Nigel froze with his spoon still halfway into the ice cream.

Discontent...in Darcy? Against her dad? Talk about new territory. And a landmine of problems if he so much as breathed wrong. "What do you want, Darcy?" He shoved the spoon into his mouth to keep from saying more. Or asking more. Because if he kept going, he'd tell her that she had every right to live her life the way she wanted, doing the job—or jobs—God had intended for her. Her dad was entitled to his opinion, just as Nigel had his, and Darcy deserved the chance to do what made her happy...even if that meant working three different jobs because she enjoyed them.

"I don't know." A deep breath punctuated the words. "I'm happy with what I do, but I don't want to disappoint him. You know how much money he's shelled out for me to take all these classes. I can't quit without getting a degree in *something*."

"Even if you spend the rest of your life in a job you hate?"

Silence answered for several heavy heartbeats before Darcy propped her head against the back of the couch and groaned. "I don't know. I should. I'm twenty-six and I have no idea what I want to do for the rest of my life. It's pitiful, really."

"No. You have to stop thinking like that. Just because you haven't known what you wanted to do since you were in kindergarten doesn't matter." Nigel struggled with the words he wanted to say. They'd been locked up so long inside the vault of his heart and mind, letting them out into the light of day felt like sacrilege. "This is your life. I'm not saying do whatever makes you happy. Sometimes our lives aren't happy. But I don't think your dad would want you working a job that made you miserable because you thought it would make him happy."

The convoluted mess twisted his brain into knots, and he stood to pace across the small cottage, leaving the ice cream melting on the table. "I suppose I'm not making much sense. What I'm trying to say is that your dad loves you. He's trying to protect you." Defending the man who stood between Nigel and his happily ever after galled him to no end, but he knew the words were true. "I'm sure if you told him how you feel, he'd understand."

Darcy's gaze followed him as he stalked across the room, met the window, turned, and headed back again. When she stepped in front of him, he jerked to a stop and shoved both hands into his pockets. "What would you do? What's your perfect job? Because I know working as Pirate Davy Jones isn't who you really are in here." She patted his chest, her small hand covering his heart.

"If I tell you, you'll change your major again." Nigel offered a lopsided grin to counter Darcy's huff.

"You're probably right." She tugged his shirt, moving toward the couch. "Now, since you're so smart, explain the rest of this to me."

Nigel returned to his corner and scooped up the nearly melted chocolate goo while Darcy rattled off a string of directions.

8

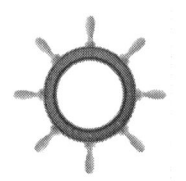

Walking backward in the sand with her hands clenched around the paddleboard bright and early on Saturday morning, Darcy muffled her disgust behind gritted teeth. Although she adored sunrise in all its beautiful majesty, forcing her eyes to open and her body to function at this early hour seemed to require its own force of nature. And she'd left her coffee at home. Too early. What possessed people to traipse through sand at this ungodly hour? Even the sun couldn't be convinced to peek over the horizon except in the most languishing portrayal of golden light.

Another grunt and yank moved the board an inch. Her breath rushed out with a guttural "Argh!" before a hand reached over her shoulder, the work-worn palm as familiar as the scratches and scars on her own arms, mementos earned through the years of working with rowdy animals with more teeth and claws than sense. Nigel's left hand landed on her shoulder as the right tugged her hot pink and white striped paddleboard from the mini Cooper's hatchback.

When she tried to step back and give him room, Darcy's foot snagged on Nigel's ankle, sending her careening off to the side.

Without missing a beat, Nigel's arm slid from her shoulder to her waist and pulled her upright. Her spine popped in protest against the sudden movement, and she yelped.

Nigel's fingers tightened for a second before he released her and used both hands to move her board toward the water. "Coffee in the truck." His head nodded toward the 4x4 parked less than fifty yards away.

Coffee. Her heart gave a pitter-pat of appreciation and her taste buds flared to life before her eyebrows scrunched together and her mouth puckered. "What are you doing out here this early?"

"And a good morning to you too. I'd almost forgotten how much you abhor waking up before sunrise." Her board fell with a *thunk*, and Nigel turned his back to her. "I was finishing up my morning run when I saw you pull in." He swiped a hand through his hair, his chest expanding with a deep breath.

"And you happen to have coffee for me?"

"No. I happen to have coffee for *me* that I've not touched, and you seem to need it more than me right now."

She couldn't see his expression, but tension surrounded him as certain as the waves bringing in the tide. Her hands fisted in the thin material of her cover-up, the only protection she needed against Elnora's summer mornings. In an hour, maybe less, she'd be grateful to discard even that slim protection as she paddled across the blue water in her modest one-piece swimsuit. Heat scattered across her face when Nigel wheeled to face her.

Something in his face turned her voice shy compared to the woman who'd faced down innumerable irate customers. "Have I done something wrong?" The change left her disconcerted.

Nigel's face collapsed into a mask. What she referred to as his Davy Jones persona. The man he portrayed on pirate tours and the façade Nigel put in place to shield his soft heart. "Not at all. Just realizing how late it is. I should be going. Work and all that."

"You'll be at the bonfire tonight, won't you?"

He waved a hand and toed the sand while staring somewhere near her collarbone. His shoulders lifted in another deep inhale before he turned again. "Sure. See ya, Darcy." He jogged away, his blue sneakers kicking up sand with every step but no Shep running alongside. He really must have been in a hurry if he'd left his furry friend at home.

Now she regretted not taking up his offer of coffee. Her system could use an energy jolt, even though a strange hum seemed to run through her veins like sand in an hourglass.

Darcy crossed her arms and inhaled the rich scent of morning dew and saltwater. Nigel's truck rumbled to a start, and he bounced away while throwing out one last wave. Mel topped the gentle rise in Zeke's truck with Mallory in the passenger seat and their paddleboards sticking over the tailgate. She slowed to a stop, Nigel doing the same, and a brief conversation ensued under Darcy's glare. So, he wouldn't talk to her, but he'd talk to Mel? Her grip tightened on her biceps until her nails dug into the tender skin and forced her to let go.

Jealousy gave a vicious jab and drove her hands to her hips. Her fingertips drummed a beat. What could Nigel tell Mel that he couldn't tell Darcy? With a huff, she tossed her head and rolled her eyes. *Stop acting like a jealous girlfriend. Jeez. Nigel's been friends with Mel as long as you. Take it down a notch.*

Drawing her gaze away from the twin trucks, Darcy snagged her board from the sand and began hauling it toward the water after strapping the Velcro strip around her left ankle. She settled the board in the water and lowered her weight onto her knees. Paddle in both hands, she eased her way over the incoming waves and out to calmer water. Mel and Mallory would catch up. Being better paddleboarders gave her friends an advantage and drove Darcy to try harder each time they made this venture. Sometimes Pen, Kendall, and the others joined in, but today it was the three of them.

Ten minutes later, Mel appeared on Darcy's left, with Mallory closing in on the other side. "You're getting faster." Mel poked Darcy with her paddle and grinned.

Mallory slapped hair from her eyes and nearly dropped her paddle.

"Not fast enough." Darcy grunted and flipped her paddle into the water. "And I still can't get to my feet without falling off a few times first."

"Better is still better." Mel shrugged one well-toned shoulder and pointed with her paddle. "Feel like going about a mile out? I saw dolphins this morning on the way over. They might still be there."

Darcy followed the pointed line, and the bridge between Hopper and Elnora came into view in the distance. She gulped past the shiver of fear dancing along her spine. "You sure it's just dolphins?" Shark attacks might be slim, practically unheard of here, but she'd rather not push her luck…or her life. Even the Bible mentioned pushing God, and Darcy had a heavy inclination that putting herself in the midst of shark-infested waters might be toeing that line.

"I'm sure." Mel frowned, the expression almost comical beneath her wide sunglasses since it made her markedly similar to the grumpy cat memes. "But if you'd rather not chance it, I understand."

"No." Darcy dug her paddle into the water and angled herself toward the bridge. "I believe you, but you know how afraid I am of sharks." She paddled ahead for a couple strokes before Mel appeared again.

Mallory continued to battle her curls, brushing them from her face only to have them reappear before she could dip her paddle into the water. "Either of you bring an extra hair tie?"

Darcy shook her head while Mel answered, "I forgot mine

too. We'll all be looking like tumbleweeds by the time we hit land."

"Oh, don't even. You two with your perfect beach waves that look like you spent hours in the salon when you rolled out of bed that way." Mallory scowled, but another riot of curls whipped around. Picking hair from between her lips, Mallory huffed. "I'm dunking my head in the water. It's the only way I'll be able to see where I'm going."

Her board bumped against Darcy's, nearly sending her overboard. Mallory grinned, then pressed her lips together when another strand fought the wind. Slick as an eel, Mallory dropped into the water and doused her hair. When she climbed back on her board, she gave a triumphant grin. "There. It'll look like I've electrocuted myself when it dries, but at least I can see."

Mel swiped her paddle through the water, sending a spray crashing over Darcy. "Let's go see dolphins!" She hopped to her feet, the move so elegant Darcy wanted to either puke or push Mel from the board. She opted for neither. At least, not yet.

Focusing on her core, Darcy tried to follow the steps Mel had given her last time. Paddle resting across the board. Hands across the paddle. Right foot up, knee bent. As her left foot came forward, she wobbled and nearly tipped into the water. Quickly righting her overextended arms, Darcy quieted her thundering heart and moved her left foot in a smooth slide until both feet were firm on the board and she crouched with knees bent and the paddle in her white-knuckled hands.

Deep breath in, and she stood upright. Her legs quivered, rocking the paddleboard until she straightened her legs and locked her core. After years of riding horses, paddleboarding should have been easier. At least she'd managed to stand on the first try. Mel was right. Better was better. Even this small improvement caused a wide smile to break through her concentration.

Mel pumped her arms overhead, the paddle moving up and

down. "Yeah, girl! You did it." She paddled alongside with smooth strokes and nodded. For a second, she seemed to want to reach over and pat Darcy's shoulder before she changed her mind and grinned.

Mallory, already on her feet, glided alongside. "And just in time. I see fins ahead."

Darcy startled, her body jerking in the direction Mallory indicated. Before she could correct, momentum and gravity took over. She landed in the water with a screech and a splash. She came up spluttering and slapping saltwater from her eyes.

Mel dropped to a cross-legged position on her board and covered her mouth with one hand.

Mallory squeaked out an "Are you all right?" before she collapsed into laughter.

"Go ahead and laugh." Darcy draped both arms over her board, content to kick her feet and recover for a moment. Her paddle floated nearby but began drifting away with every passing second. Darcy pushed off from her board and struck out toward the wayward object. Grasping it with one hand, she turned again toward her board. The ankle strap kept it tethered and almost within reach. Before she could touch the slick epoxy, something bumped her leg. A scream erupted before she could swallow the panic.

Mel's belly-deep laughter ceased, and a frown took over. "What? What happened?"

"Something touched my leg!" Darcy scrambled onto her board and held her paddle overhead like a club. Seconds later, a fin broke the surface. Darcy shot backwards, almost tumbling off the end of her board before her brain recognized the curved dorsal fin as belonging to a dolphin. She released a gusty sigh and clapped a hand to her heart when the dolphin's nose appeared near the front of her board.

Mel eased forward, the sound of her gasp louder than Darcy's galloping heart. "Look at that. They're still here." She crouched low and her hand crept forward. "You think it's okay to touch them?"

"They're wild animals, Mel." But even Darcy couldn't deny the sudden itch in her palms at the thought of touching a dolphin. Some people wanted to swim with sharks. The very idea froze her insides. Dolphins, though, what islander didn't dream of dolphins?

Mallory tucked her board in close and peered into the water. "How many you think there are?"

"I count five fins." Mel's hand continued sliding forward. "And how many times have you been bitten or scratched by tame animals, Darcy? I don't think I can pass this up."

"Point taken. But that also pushes the point. Even tame animals are capable of harm. Wild animals even more so."

The dolphin ignored their conversation and chattered in their funny clicking language. A row of sharp teeth stilled Darcy, and Mel hesitated. When the dolphin disappeared beneath the surface, Darcy nearly sighed. Disappointment seeped through, shattering the moment.

Mel paddled in a slow circle, obviously looking for more fins. "There were more earlier. At least six. Maybe they'll be back."

"There's one." Mallory pointed, then squealed when another dolphin bumped against her board, sending her into the ocean with an open-armed splash. Her laughter bubbled out as she broke the surface and wiped hair from her eyes. "Guess I could have saved myself that first dunk."

They spent the next hour paddling alongside the dolphin pod. The curious creatures never seemed to mind and often rolled sideways to give each of them a long, steady look. Mel ran her hand across the dorsal fin of their chatty friend and beamed a kilowatt smile.

The most curious of the bunch continued to chatter every time it breached the surface. Darcy forced calmness into her adrenaline-driven system and reached out her hand. How often would she get this opportunity? In twenty-six years of island life, she'd never been this close to a dolphin. Some opportunities might never come again, and she wouldn't want fear to keep her from something so amazing.

When the dolphins bored of them, the pod swam away with a flash of dorsal fins and tail flukes before two decided to put on a show. Leaping into the air, they flew over each other and seemed to smile before disappearing below.

The trio paddled back to shore in silence, unwilling to break the moment, until another familiar face appeared on the beach. "Isn't that Ben Hornigold?" Darcy shielded her eyes and squinted, trying to make certain of the man's identity.

Mallory reached for her hair, which had grown to the size of a show-stopping French poodle. "Oh, no. My hair." She raked her fingers into the curls but was forced to give up when her frenzied actions only made her yelp. "Distract him. I'll be right back."

"Bit late for that since we're all coming in at the same time." Mel gave a Cheshire cat grin. "Oh, look…he's waving." She threw up her arm. "Morning, Ben!"

9

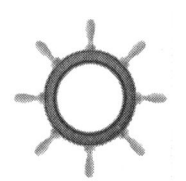

A long row of bonfires dotted the stretch of Elnora beach, each one sending sparks soaring into the pitch-black sky. No moon shone, but stars filled the sky, tiny lights shining as a reminder of God's infinite love and mercy.

A reminder Darcy desperately needed. God's time was not her time. He would do things His way, and her life would be better for it, if only she could let go and let Him do the work. Her chilled fingers fisted inside her hoodie pocket. *God, help me to be patient.*

Mel waved to her from the nearest bonfire. But Nigel's blocky shadow had more appeal. Mel snuggled against Zeke's side. As much as Darcy loved the vivacious dog groomer, she wouldn't be a third wheel to Mel's romantic moment. From the nod Zeke offered, he thanked Darcy for walking by without stopping. The look in his eye sent an arrow of awareness darting through her bloodstream. She'd seen that look too many times from sweating boyfriends on the cusp of proposal.

Dropping onto the blanket beside Nigel, Darcy reached into the nearby cooler and pulled out a water bottle. "Zeke's gonna propose."

"Nah." Nigel batted at a spark flying too near his beard, but his head swiveled toward the couple on their left. "You really think?"

"Wait and see." Leaning back and crossing her ankles, she shivered at the sudden gust of wind. "Shoulda changed into some pants. I know better than to come down here at nighttime in shorts."

"It's the middle of summer." Nigel reached into his backpack and pulled out a fuzzy maroon blanket. "Only you would get cold in the middle of summer while sitting beside a blazing fire. I'm about to melt over here."

Darcy caught the blanket with one hand and spread it out over her legs. They had the same argument every time. But he never stopped bringing her an extra blanket, and she never stopped expecting him to.

When he dropped another log onto the bonfire, she caught the tic of his left eyelid. Something had annoyed him. Nigel kept his emotions bottled up under lock and key. Scratch that. He shoved them into a chest, wrapped them in chains, closed it with a padlock, and sank the chest in the middle of the ocean like some precious treasure. No one ever saw the man break. He took cool, calm, and collected to the nth degree. Something that often infuriated Darcy and drove her to see how much it would take to see Nigel unlock his heart.

In the twenty years they'd known each other, nothing had ever worked. The closest she ever came would be to have him explain what caused that one eyelid to flutter in rhythmic spasms. She wasn't in the mood for sensitive today. "What's got your eye in a knot?"

Nigel placed one finger against the spot still pulsing every few seconds and shook his head. "Work stuff." As though to defy the lie, his eye twitched again. When he tucked his head down and crossed his arms, Darcy moved around the fire to sit beside him.

"Liar, liar, pants on fire." She motioned at the sparks floating around them like deranged lightning bugs. "And I really could set your pants on fire. So, stop being a macho man and tell me the truth."

Before he could give in to inevitability, Zeke's low voice reached her ears. Darcy put her hand on Nigel's shoulder and squeezed. He frowned at her hand but didn't move away like he often did.

"Mel, I know we've not even been dating a year yet, but I love you." Zeke chuckled and clutched Mel's hands in his. "I'll confess, I've worked through this a hundred times, but nothing ever comes out right. I've written business proposals and grant proposals, but proposing to you..." A deep sigh lingered several beats. "There are no words. Working with you all those days hunting for Daphne, it awakened a dream I didn't know I wanted. What I'm trying to say, and failing miserably, is, Melody Carmichael, will you marry me?" Somewhere in the fluctuation of love speak, Zeke pulled a ring from his pocket, and he presented it to Mel with a flourish as he rolled up to one knee.

Even in the firelight, the ring twinkled as though it knew the occasion.

Mel's yes reached dog-whistle levels, the decibel screaming past ear-splitting and going straight into the stratosphere. She threw her arms around Zeke's neck with what could only be joyful sobs.

"I'll assume that's a yes." Zeke's voice muffled against Mel's neck until she leaned back and wiped away her tears while her head bobbed.

Darcy dashed tears away from her own eyes. Nigel squeezed her hand, having taken it into his own sometime during the process. Heat razed her fingers and traveled up her arm, replaced with a chill when he released her hand and reached for another piece of driftwood to place on the fire.

"You were right." The dark octave in his voice drew her gaze to his face, where a deep frown had taken up residence.

She sniffed and dried her eyes on her sleeve. "Aren't you happy? I've seen a dozen proposals this month, but that's got to be the best one so far. It's perfect for them after all the time they spent searching the beach last year."

"But it wasn't Elnora's beach they searched." Nigel's eyebrows furrowed. "I would think it would have more impact on Merriweather."

"You're making it too complicated, Nigel. It's the heart of the matter that counts. Zeke knows Mel, and it showed."

"Yeah? So, your perfect proposal would be, what? Midnight at the lighthouse?"

Something flickered across his expression, there and gone again before she could identify the minute changes. Firelight hindered her plundering gaze, but the blasted tic had resumed its beat in his eyelid. His beard hid the rest, but she'd almost been certain he'd seemed pained.

She injected a modicum of self-depreciation into her tone, along with a heavy dose of fake optimism. "Nah. I've decided to become a spinster. I'll travel the world, never settling down. Always on the hunt for my next grand adventure."

Nigel snorted, reminding her of Patches after a trying day at the stables. He worked his feet into the sand but never turned her way.

"What? You don't believe me?" She shoved his arm, knocking him off balance and sideways into the sand. Confound it all. She wanted his approval for this decision. His opinion mattered… more than most. Nigel always had her back. He'd been the only one to take her side in sixth grade when she decided that vanilla was no longer an ice cream flavor and she needed a new favorite. Having him hold out on her now was worse than torture.

Righting himself, he withered her smile with a long glare.

His jaw ticked to some tune only he could hear. Eyes bright in the firelight but burning with some inner turmoil she couldn't decipher, he released a breath. "If that's what you truly want, I'll support you. If that's the task God's given you, I'll not stand in your way. But if this is you pitching a pity party because every Tom, Dick, and Harry you've dated lately has been less than ideal? No."

Something warm and tingly settled in her stomach. Like the moment when a little kid realizes the puppy in the box is for them. Or when a mother sees the ultrasound for the first time. Hope. Warm and beautiful. It washed through her in gentle waves, each one shoring up her broken confidence and sending her dreams to new heights.

"You were meant to love and be loved. You, more than anyone I know, deserve to be a wife and a mother." His words spread like honey on a biscuit over her tattered heart, stitching over the bad memories with his assurance.

This was the Nigel she knew. Her champion. The one person she could count on to never let her down and to always know what to say when she needed it most. "It's no wonder you're my best friend."

"Yeah, well…" Nigel paused and turned his head, coughing into his elbow. His voice turned hoarse when he continued, "Don't spread the word. I'd hate to ruin my reputation."

"You okay?"

After he took a swig of water, he nodded. "Fine. I think I'm gonna head home. Your dad had me pull an extra shift today, and I'm beat."

Darcy nodded and stretched out on the blanket. "I'll bring your stuff by later."

10

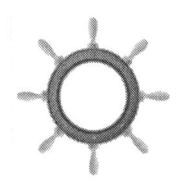

If he didn't know better, Nigel would swear he'd been poisoned. After the bonfire, he'd gone home only to collapse in bed...where he'd remained all day Sunday. This morning, he'd managed to drag himself into the living room, but he only made it as far as the couch.

The pounding in his head matched the thumping knock radiating from the front door. Nigel pressed his palm against the right side of his face and opened the door a crack. Even that tiny movement sent a shaft of daylight piercing straight into his skull. Through squinted eyes, he caught a glimpse of Darcy standing on his tiny stoop with a yellow Dutch oven cradled in her hands.

When he tried to speak, a hacking cough forced him to double over with one hand to his head and the other against his chest.

Darcy pushed her way inside, his flagging strength unable to keep a fly out of a window, much less a grown woman away from his door.

"Go sit down before you fall down." Darcy headed toward his kitchen after nudging the door closed with her toe. "I'll be back in two minutes, and you'd better be on that couch or I'll put you under it." Her curt order and the sassy swing of her hips said she meant business.

Since standing took too much effort anyway, Nigel collapsed on the couch, right where he'd been when nurse Darcy arrived. Tugging the flannel blanket over his legs and torso, Nigel slowly reached for the glass of lemonade that had grown warm hours ago but wasn't worth getting up to replace.

Darcy reappeared, hands on hips and a frown pinching her lips together. "How long have you been sick?"

Nigel opened his mouth to reply he'd be fine when another barking cough sucked every morsel of oxygen from his lungs. Fire raced from his chest and spread up his throat, the dry hack producing nothing but a red face and dry gagging.

He expected Darcy to flinch away from the unpleasant expression he'd seen covering his face when he happened past a mirror while coughing, but she simply hummed and reached into her pocket. A box of cold and flu tablets appeared in her palm. A wonderful commodity to have if he'd been able to travel the miles between himself and the store. Who was he kidding? Just the few feet between him and Darcy stretched further than his current endurance. The small grocery store downtown might as well be on another continent.

"You realize you could have texted me? Because your thumbs can't cough." She waved the package in his direction. "I can't believe you would sit here a whole day and not ask anyone for help. You're such a guy." She threw the orange and white box, landing it perfectly on his stomach, and stomped back into the kitchen.

He'd chuckle if it wouldn't hurt so badly and start another round of coughing. Keeping his cough/cold crud to himself had been the highest priority. Not to mention today was the first day he'd seen daylight for more than a few seconds at a time. Whatever he had, it had bundled up every ounce of strength he possessed and run away to the far reaches of the earth. Even opening the paper box had him breathing hard. Who made these decisions to package critical medicine in a box glued shut with super adhesive glue *after* wrapping those gorgeous relief-inducing pills in impenetrable plastic? If he made it to the plastic, he'd likely break his teeth trying to rip through the stinking stuff.

Darcy came back with a pair of scissors in one hand and a glass of water in the other. She pointed the scissors at him. "Don't you dare bite that and get your nasty germs all over everything. Give it here. I only meant for you to hold it, not mutilate it." She slid the blade into the box and pried out a dose of medicine. After slicing through the packaging, she freed his relief in the form of glistening orange horse-sized pills and dropped them into his waiting palm.

He tried to smile his thanks, but his neck hurt too much to allow the full movement. With the glass of ice-cold water in one hand and the meds in the other, he forced his head up far enough to toss the pills in and follow it with a gulp of liquid. The water sent a shiver down his backbone. Chills had wracked him for the last twenty-four hours, best he could tell. His phone had died yesterday and finding the charger had been beyond his range of motion.

Darcy continued to glower, but the scowl diminished somewhat when he sighed and gave her a thumbs-up.

"Can you not talk at all?"

He shook his head and winced.

Her hands popped back onto her hips. "Tell me the truth. Are you sick sick or man-flu sick?"

Before he could make a motion to prove his inability to answer a two-part question, another cough did the job for him. When it ended, he was leaning forward, chest pressed against his thighs and palms holding up a head that felt like it weighed a hundred pounds. Darcy sat beside him, though when she'd moved, he couldn't say.

"Well, that answers one question anyway." She rubbed circles on his back. "Can you answer me with a thumbs-up if you have a symptom and thumbs-down if you don't?"

Thumbs-up.

"Good." Another circle of her hand across his back. "So, nonproductive cough, check. Based on the heat coming through your shirt right now, I'm guessing fever. Have you checked your temperature?"

Thumbs-down.

"Okay. We'll worry about that in a minute. After that much coughing, checking it now won't give me an accurate number. Headache?"

Thumbs-up. As she rattled off a list: sore throat, aches, chills, nausea, he kept his thumb in the air. When she moved on to bowel issues, he dropped his thumb and began waving his other hand to stop the line of questioning.

"Okay." Her hand left his back. "I'm going to heat up the soup and call Dr. Roberts. I think you have bronchitis, but I can't be sure."

He wanted to try and object but lacked the energy. Instead, he closed his eyes and leaned into the pile of pillows Darcy had insisted he needed when he moved into his cottage. She'd promised the cream-colored pillows with blue anchors were too perfect to pass up. At the time, he'd complained his house would be fine without frippery—using the word to tick Darcy off—but he could admit they came in handy for a nap.

What felt like minutes later, his own snoring jolted him out of unconsciousness. His head lolled to the side, revealing Darcy sitting on the far end of the sofa with his socked feet in her lap. She had one fist on his calf, using his leg as a table for what looked like a cup of coffee. He couldn't breathe well enough to sniff and know for certain. In her other hand, a familiar green folder lay open.

At his garbled grunt, she glanced over but didn't move. Heat from the cup warmed his leg where it had escaped the worn flannel blanket.

"Did you write this?" Her gaze speared him and heat a thousand times hotter than his worst fever infused his face and neck. "Nigel, it's wonderful. I had no idea you could write. Well. I mean, I knew you could write. We went to school together, after all. But this," she waved her hand over the binder filled with pages and pages of handwritten words. "I didn't know you could do this. Have you sent it to anyone?"

A wince from him seemed to be enough. He lacked the breath to say no one had ever read his work before. And no one would be reading it now if he'd not fallen ill in the middle of writing the final pages of the third book in the series. Darcy held the first volume, which he'd pulled from the shelf to reference while working with characters who made appearances throughout the trilogy. Seeing it there, the green suede soft against her skin, set off fireworks of irrational fear. She'd already said the book was good. Her face lacked the scattered look of a lie, and her eyes continued to dart back toward the page as though attempting to snag another word.

Closing the book with a soft slap, Darcy stood, likely leaving now that she knew he'd survive another day. "You missed your soup. I'll heat another bowl." She reached down and brushed her fingers over his forehead. "Your fever's broken, so maybe you can stay awake for more than five minutes this time. You have medicine you need to take."

The word formed on his lips but refused to pass. Medicine? He quirked his eyebrows, pleading for an explanation. Confound his noodle-like strength. If he could swing around, the pad of paper and a dozen pens sat on Darcy's end of the sofa. He could at least write out his questions.

Darcy pressed a palm to his chest. "I called the doc. Gave him your symptoms and he did a virtual exam. He's certain you've managed to give yourself bronchitis. Called in some meds to the pharmacy and I picked them up while you were passed out." She grinned and tweaked his beard, sending a thrill through his body. "You never even missed me. Too busy sawing every tree in the forest into kindling."

"Thank you." His voice rumbled like an asthmatic smoker, but he managed to rasp those two words together without coughing up either lung.

"Yeah, yeah. Now stop talking." Darcy grinned. "This could be fun. If you can stay awake, we should play some card games."

Widening his eyes, Nigel attempted to convey his desire to stay awake. If Darcy wanted to stay and play nurse, he'd let her.

11

Rummaging through the drawers in Nigel's kitchen, Darcy finally scrounged up a deck of playing cards. He'd redecorated since the last time she'd been here. The cabinets were now powder-blue instead of white. Clean dishes lined the shelves, and the rickety kitchen table had been replaced with a farmhouse chic butcher block with white legs. When had he done this?

A frown tugged her lips. When was the last time she'd been here? A year ago? That couldn't be right. She saw Nigel at least three times a week. Until lately. These past few months had been crazy, but that shouldn't have affected them this much.

Shuffling the cards into one hand, she ladled out a bowl of homemade chicken noodle soup and carried it back to the living room where Nigel waited with his eyes pried open.

There was something endearing about his wide-eyed but relaxed posture. Like a little boy waiting for Christmas even though he's so worn out his body demanded sleep. She should let him sleep. His recovery would benefit.

As though he read her expression, Nigel leaned forward, pushing himself up from the mound of cushions and reaching for the bowl she still held. He nodded when she passed it over, probably too afraid of the wracking cough to talk.

His color improved with each bite of rich broth until he looked almost normal. Almost. After spending so many years onboard the *Treasure,* Nigel's normal swarthy complexion looked washed-out with illness. Seeing him like this, weak and dependent, made her insides squirm. Nigel never needed anyone for anything. Having him look at her as though she'd done the best thing ever…well, it felt good.

Moving back to his side, she cleared the coffee table, shifting his book in the process. Another shocker. Nigel as an author. He'd be magnificent. Even the unpublished rough draft she'd seen peeking out from beneath the circular, pine coffee table and read nearly a hundred pages of was one of the best stories she'd read in a long time. A million questions stomped through her mind. It'd do her no good to ask them since Nigel could barely croak out two words. One of these days, she'd demand he give her the full story. But not today. She wasn't completely heartless. He could recover for a few days before she pounced.

"I think we can play Go Fish without too much trouble." Darcy shuffled the cards several times before dealing out the allotted amount for each of them. "Instead of asking me if I have something, just show me the card. To keep it fair, I'll do the same thing. It's like quiet as a mouse and a card game at the same time."

Nigel grinned and picked up his cards. The expression said he didn't believe she could be quiet for an entire game.

He was probably right.

Fanning her cards out, Darcy waved her hand. "You go first."

He smirked and held up a seven.

Her mouth opened and a "ggg" emerged before she snapped her trap shut and shook her head.

Nigel's shoulders lifted in silent mirth even as his mouth

twisted in a grimace. He pulled another card into his hand before pointing at her.

The game continued with silence pressing upon them like a weighted blanket. Comforting and familiar. When it ended, Darcy handed Nigel his prescribed medications and carried the dirty dishes to the kitchen. He could hardly keep his eyes open by the time she washed up the empty bowls and returned.

"I'll be back in the morning." She took the spare key from the key box beside the front door and tucked it into her pocket. "Where's your phone?"

Nigel pointed down the hallway, then slashed his hand across his neck.

"Your battery's dead?"

A nod.

"Where's your charger?"

Nigel held his hands out in clenched fists, positioned at ten and two. He rotated them from side to side as though driving.

"In the truck?"

He tapped his finger against his nose and winked. Only the wink turned into a long blink, followed by a yawn.

"Go to sleep, Nigel." Darcy tucked the blanket over his shoulders and brushed curls away from his gorgeous gray eyes. "I'll put your phone on the table beside you and plug it in to charge. Call me if you need anything before morning." His face flushed beneath her hands, but he nodded and pressed his cheek into her palm for a brief second.

When his eyes closed again, she rubbed her fingers over her tingling palm. The strange reaction of Nigel's beard against her hand raced up her arm. She reached out, intending to touch him again, but jerked her hand back at the last second. He needed rest. And she needed to get herself under control. This was Nigel. Her best friend. Not a boyfriend. Not someone she had any romantic feelings for. Not at all.

But that didn't mean she couldn't come back in the morning and keep house for him.

Returning to her own cottage, she found her parents settled in matching beach chairs on her deck. Her dad stood when she approached and sent a long look over her shoulder. "You've been at Nigel's."

It wasn't a question. The dark tone indicated disapproval, and Darcy tensed her shoulders. "He's sick. I took over some soup and made sure he had medicine." Sending a hopeful look at her mother, asking for help, Darcy opened the door and ushered them inside. "What are you two doing all the way down here?"

"You weren't answering your phone, so we came down to check on you." Her mother embraced Darcy's shoulders and squeezed. "It's been so long since you came to visit. We miss our girl."

"And it's a good thing we did. Darcy, I don't think it's wise for you to spend so much time alone with Nigel."

"Dad." She gave an inward groan. "Nigel has been my friend since we were six. You can't expect me to sit around and ignore him, especially when he's sick. He could barely walk through the house, much less manage to get food for himself."

Pausing inside the living room, her dad smoothed his hands over the black tie tucked neatly into his blazer. "So, you put yourself at risk to care for him. You know better. Nigel can fend for himself. He's a big boy, and he doesn't need you hovering over him every minute of the day."

"It's not like I have anything else to do." She worried her lip to keep from blurting out that taking care of Nigel had helped her somehow.

Her mother patted Darcy's arm and reached for her husband. "Well, dear, now that we know Darcy's not kidnapped or some such, why don't we head back home. Darcy, you're welcome to join us for supper. I've a lovely roast in the Crock-Pot."

Not one to let her mother or anyone else have the last word, her dad leaned forward and pointed a finger. "Just remember, men like Nigel Jones are likely to take off and disappear. Don't put your hopes in him. Find yourself a proper man. Not one without ambition like your friend." He made friend sound like something dirty when he sneered. "I've known men like Nigel before. They're no good."

"Yes, yes." Mom steered him toward the door, her floral skirt swishing with each step. "Love you, darling."

Reaching for a strand of hair, Darcy twirled the black lock between her fingers. Her heart galloped with a mixture of anger and amusement. Good ol' Dad. Always pushing for her to do better. Be better.

But I won't give up my best friend. No matter what you think. Tossing her head, she stomped to her bedroom and fell across the bed.

She barged through Nigel's front door the next morning as though she owned the place. And she might as well at this point. Nigel lay sprawled across the sofa, one foot on the floor and the other across the back of the couch. His arms had made their way over his head, and a deep, bear-worthy snore practically rattled the pictures off the walls. He needed the sleep but not with that infernal noise.

Darcy grabbed a nearby pillow and hurled it at his chest. "Roll onto your side before you choke yourself."

The resulting snort and gasp for breath, along with the look of bleary shock on his face sent Darcy into a peal of laughter. "I'll be in the kitchen fixing breakfast. Sleep if you want. I'll have coffee ready soon."

"I'll stay up."

She could barely make out the mumbled words, but when he rolled upright, she understood well enough. "You might feel better if you take a shower. The steam will help with the congestion."

Nigel grunted in reply and crept toward the short hallway.

Darcy followed his progress, holding her breath until the bathroom door closed and locked. At the quiet click, apprehension pelted her insides. What if he fell in the shower? He hadn't seemed dizzy, but one never knew with the amount of congestion rattling around in his head and chest.

Her ears stayed perked for any unusual sounds while whipping up a quick breakfast of sausage biscuits with honey. She carried full mugs of coffee to the table as the bathroom door opened and Nigel's steps approached. Freshly showered, his curls dripping water onto his blue t-shirt, he looked like a bedraggled little boy. No. There was nothing little about Nigel. Not in a long time. He possessed a masculine power that drew people to him, men and women alike. She'd seen the looks from women at church. He had an easy demeanor and a cheerful attitude that made others want to be his friend.

But Nigel held everyone at arm's length. Even her. She'd been his friend longer than most. When was the last time he'd asked her for anything? Asked for her help or her advice? Ever? She couldn't think of a single example.

Quickly settling into her seat, Darcy picked up her coffee and motioned for him to join her. "I'll have to work the next few days, but I'll check in on you when I can."

"Got to go to work tomorrow." He sounded like he'd eaten sandpaper for supper and nails for a midnight snack. When he cleared his throat and went into a coughing fit, he pounded his chest and winced. "No vacation time left with the summer camp coming up. Need to work."

"You can't, Nigel."

"Can. Bronchitis isn't contagious. I googled it." He gave her a glare that said he wouldn't be swayed and picked up his coffee.

"But you can't sing. You're too worn out to perform any of

the dances. What'll you do?"

"Cap…" A cough seized him, bending him over the table, head in his hands. Wheezing, he wiped a hand over his face, removing the strain before he tried again. "Captain says I can work the booth. Savannah will do the talking."

Oh, goodie. Her face attempted to betray the ragged jealousy. Blonde and perfect, Savannah had been trying to catch Nigel's eye all summer.

"Are you ready for summer camp?" Darcy swirled her cup, eyes riveted on Nigel for any sign she needed to lock him in the house and throw away the key. He needed to recover. And she needed a distraction from the idea of Nigel and Savannah cooped up in the tiny booth for hours on end.

Nigel gave her a cheeky grin, only slightly altered by a convulsive swallow. "Wouldn't miss it for the world." He hesitated before pushing his full plate off to the side. "Thank you for everything you've done, Darcy." He gave her a side smile. "I know you love taking care of me, but I'll be okay."

Yes, he would. Nigel always bounced back. Most times with an even bigger spring in his step. Insufferable man.

Gathering her dishes, Darcy headed to the sink to clean up before she left for work. "I guess I'll see you next week for camp then." She scrubbed the dishes—with more force than necessary—while Nigel picked through the food on his plate. He probably didn't have much of an appetite, but his refusal to eat made it feel like a personal rejection.

He looked up when she clanged her coffee cup against her plate before dropping it into the dishwasher. "What? What's wrong?"

"Nothing." She swiped her hands over a dishtowel and reached for her bag. "See you later."

Nigel's gaze bore into her back with every step, but she couldn't look back. Not with her emotions crashing and burning all over her face.

12

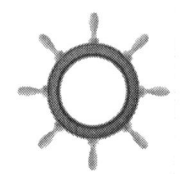

The week at camp flew faster than any other. Nigel kept so busy with the teens he only caught passing glances of Darcy. Peering down from the *Seabound*'s crow's nest, Nigel had a perfect view of Darcy as she danced around the deck with the gaggle of kids. Their annual summer camp had started out with a random thunderstorm, keeping them confined in their cabins.

After that short outburst, mother nature had been kind, and the kids had spent the rest of the week discovering, exploring, and learning. Nestled safe and secure in a protected cove off Skye's shore, the crew of counselors had kept the kids entertained and relatively calm during the storm and gave them ample excursions through the week.

Sunshine every day kissed their skin despite layers of sunscreen. Nigel enjoyed the deepening tan covering his face and arms. Soon, he'd be surfing, and the tan would take over most of his body. He took precautions against permanent damage, but some sun could not be avoided. Likewise, Darcy had become sun-kissed, her freckles popping out. She would grumble about them later, but Nigel didn't mind the dots sprinkled like stars across her nose. They would be heading back today, another week well spent with this group of almost adults.

With their final day reaching its end, Captain, crew, and kids had boarded the ship for their journey home. Nigel hoped they could one day have these same summer camps aboard ship. They were in no more danger on the *Seabound* than in cabins on land. With nothing nearby to knock holes in *Seabound*, they could anchor in this same cove and give the kids a taste of life as it might have been two hundred years ago.

Nigel leaned his forearms on the wooden rail, his attention drawn to the flashes of color and squeals of laughter.

One of the crew, Steven, worked his accordion like a master, pumping a lively tune across the deck for the whirling dancers. Several more kids joined their hands to the circle, moving around Darcy. She twirled in a full circle, her skirt spinning in a golden arc as it picked up sunbeams, seeming to soak them up and create a glow that spread across her face. Radiant. She'd never been more beautiful than in that moment of pure child-like joy.

George Tanner crossed his arms and scowled from his position at the rail. George had remained recalcitrant all week, sullen, and flat out surly at times. In previous years, his friend Caleb had managed to help bring the younger boy out of his shell. With Caleb graduated and living with his uncle in Alabama, George had been left without any other close friends. Nigel had hoped this week might prompt some new friendships to develop before school began in a few months. George had done his best to keep everyone from getting more than a grunt as an answer to any question. Not the best way to build lasting friendships.

Swinging out of the nest, Nigel scrambled down the rigging and landed directly beside George. "Ready to go home?"

A scowl and a shrug met Nigel's question. Undeterred, he leaned against the railing and matched George's pose. The music lifted again, soaring high enough to reach the great, puffy clouds.

George harrumphed and shoved his hands deep into oversized pockets. "Dunno why he has to play like that. Not like there's anyone to challenge him."

"Didn't you play the harmonica?" Nigel kept his gaze on Steven, but he caught the jerk of George's head in his direction before the youth blew out a long breath. Nigel let the movement go without contest, giving George the chance to decide where the conversation might go next.

Pulling his right hand from his pocket, George palmed a scarred and tarnished harmonica. "Hard to play when you sound as bad as me." A dark scowl pulled his mouth into a long frown as the wind whipped across the bow and sent Nigel's shirt snapping taut against his chest.

"Best I can remember," Nigel tapped his forehead in an old-fashioned Winnie the Pooh pose, "you were a fair player. In fact, you were asked to play at the Captain's Day parade this year."

George shrugged and returned the harmonica to his pocket. "Pity nomination. Found out last day of school. Becca put my name on the list."

"Uh-huh. And now you think that just any ol' person who gets their name on the list can be chosen to play." Nigel shook his head when George started to interrupt. "When I happen to know that you were chosen because of the way you played in the Christmas play."

"How do you know that?" Hope colored George's voice. Along with a hint of woebegone fear.

"I was on the committee." Nigel clapped George's shoulder. "Which means you need to be practicing. Captain's Day will be here before you know it. And I fully expect to see you leading the parade with the others." He left George standing open-mouthed and strode through the crowd. Looping his arm through Darcy's, Nigel swung her into a circle before joining the boot-stomping rhythm that caused the deck to shiver beneath his boots.

Minutes later, George's smooth tunes joined Steven, ratcheting the tempo up a tick and sending the dancers into a frenzy of movement. Darcy spun away, her body in perfect harmony with the music. Patrick joined the two boys, adding his spoons and deep baritone as he launched into song.

Darcy whooped and began a ring-around-the-rosy circle. Faces shining with a mixture of joy and exercise, the kids joined in until not a one remained outside the spinning mayhem.

Best camp ever.

Nigel stomped in time, the smile on his face stretching so wide his cheeks ached. He'd needed this week away from the madness of work. A week where he could be with Darcy under circumstances where they could relax. Her expression the day she left his house had haunted him until she stepped aboard and gave him a smile that said all was forgiven.

He'd suffered twelve hours elbow to elbow with Savannah—with Darcy mad at him for who-knows-what reason—fending off shoulder bumps and batting eyelashes from a woman he wouldn't date in a hundred years. At one point, she'd batted her eyes so hard, one of her fake eyelashes had fallen. He couldn't help but laugh when she jumped up, bumped her head on the roof, and slapped at her own face, while shouting something about a spider.

Darcy whirled by, snagged his elbow, and hauled him into the circle. A perfect ending for a perfect week.

13

Darcy yawned and scrubbed her eyes. Back to work with Mel on Merriweather after a week-long camp had left her equal parts exhausted and energized. Which put her body in a perpetual state of confusion and created ample opportunities for Mel to cause trouble.

Mel elbowed Darcy and wrapped the leash around her hand. Her current charge, a large, red-haired Afghan Hound named Daphne, had escaped the previous year. Since then, Mel always took extra precautions with Zeke's grandmother's dog.

"Do you ever wonder what might be different if Daphne hadn't escaped?" Darcy ruffled the dog's ears before Mel opened the mobile grooming truck's door.

Mel paused, her hand raised to shield her eyes and a smile blooming on her face. "Every day." She walked Daphne out but stopped once she reached the sidewalk leading up to Miss Evelyn's house. "I still think we would have ended up right where we are now. Some plans are simply meant to be."

"I never understood why you didn't fire me." Shoving a baseball cap over her head to tame the waves, Darcy lowered her eyes until the cover gave her a break from the sunlight. "It wasn't the first time I'd made a mistake."

"You're one of my best friends." Mel reached over to squeeze Darcy's arm before she could speak. Daphne pulled against the leash, tugging Mel toward the front door. "But that's not why I let you keep working. Can you imagine what would happen if mistakes were never forgiven? What if we made one mistake and God said, 'That's it. I'm done with you.'? Doesn't sound like the loving Father we've been brought up to trust."

"I guess my real question is, when will I stop making mistakes? I'm so tired of getting things wrong all the time. Dad's always disappointed in me. Says I spend too much time chasing frivolous dreams. He thinks I should do more with my life so I can have the perfect future he's always dreamed of."

"I don't know that any future is perfect." Mel scrunched her nose. "I'm sorry your dad puts so much pressure on you. That's got to be tough."

"Yeah. I don't get it. Why do I keep messing up?"

"Can't answer that. I mess up all the time. This morning, I poured orange juice in my oatmeal and tried to crank the truck using a padlock key. It's a wonder I didn't break something." Mel chuckled as they reached the stoop. She pressed the doorbell and waited.

Darcy's chest tightened as a biting remark threatened to leap from her mouth. The days of working at the ranch and taking control of irate customers had started building a new aspect to her personality. It had tried to shift itself into her daily life, but she refused to allow the change.

Her silence lingered through Mel handing Daphne back to her owner, all the way until they were in the truck with the air conditioning blasting and a steady beat from the radio filling the quiet.

"Okay, spill." Mel wheeled them onto the road and headed toward Elnora. She'd made Daphne their last groom of the day on Merriweather. It would only take a few more clients for Mel to have more business than one truck could handle. "We're meeting Pen at your house. You have until then to tell me why you look like you've eaten an entire bushel of lemons."

A piano rendition of "Amazing Grace" trickled over the airwaves. Darcy patted her foot to the beat and shook her head at Mel. "Nothing to tell."

"Careful there. If your pants catch on fire, I'll spray you with the fire extinguisher while dancing in a circle shouting, 'Told you so!'"

Where the irritation had burned, amusement took its place. Darcy's lips quirked, pulling the tension from her eyes at not being able to hold the frown as the memory of her and Nigel at the beach washed through her. "Ever feel like your insides are a bubbling cauldron? Like you've added one too many of the wrong ingredients and it's threatening to boil over?"

"Sounds like acid to me." Mel pulled the truck off the road and put it in park when Darcy gave a snort of protest. "That's it. Talk to me. What's going on?"

"Nothing…Everything." Darcy ripped the cap off her head and flung it against the windshield. "There's so much…something, boiling inside me. It's affecting everything. I don't feel like myself. The bubbly, happy-go-lucky Darcy has hit a brick wall and bounced off like a bowl of raw spaghetti."

"You're really into the food analogies today. Should we go somewhere and eat while we talk this over?"

"See, like that right there." Darcy spun in her seat, turning to face Mel. "A few months ago, I would have laughed and said sure. Right now, I just want to sulk. I've never been like this before. What's happening to me?"

Her friend frowned so deep a groove appeared between her eyes. "What's changed? Not in your personality. In your life. Something brought this on."

"Nothing."

Mel's eyebrows hiked up.

Darcy squeezed her thighs and rocked back against the door. The muscles in her neck spasmed and tightened into a hard knot. "I'm telling the truth. Nothing has changed. I work the same jobs. I go to the same places. My routine is as rich and glamorous as it's always been."

"Can I ask you something personal?" When she nodded, Mel continued. "Is this about you wanting to be married?"

"I don't know."

"Okay. Think about it for a minute and let me know. Because I think if you'll be honest with yourself, you'll see I'm right. You're obsessing over finding the perfect man to marry." Mel steered them back onto the road and let the silence do its work. "Even though you've said you're giving up on the whole institution of marriage."

Darcy fidgeted, then tucked her hands beneath her legs to keep from rubbing her hands together for the hundredth time. "I don't understand why it's so hard. You weren't even looking for a guy when Zeke got pushed at you. I've been looking for years. When is it my turn?" Her hands escaped and spread wide in the spacious cab. "I've been asking and praying for *years*."

They rumbled over the bridge, and Darcy turned her attention to the ocean spread out all around them. Elnora crept into view, the lush green giving her a rush of relief.

"I'm going to ask another really personal question that you don't have to answer." Mel gave the warning with a quirk of mouth in a tiny smile. "I've seen you, been close to you, on nearly a dozen dates this summer. You've rejected each one after no more than an hour."

"You said there was a question." Darcy shoved the cap back on her head and pulled the bill closer to her eyes to cover her expression.

Mel chuckled and flicked her blinker. "Right. What's your reason for rejecting them? And if you're tossing out a dozen dates in a couple months, how many are you saying no to without even meeting them?"

"Probably thirty." Darcy shrugged and shoved her hands back under her legs. "I've had different reasons for saying no to second dates."

"Examples."

Darcy's little cottage came into view. Set against the backdrop of a setting sun, she couldn't ask for anything more beautiful. "I don't remember them all." She reached for the door handle and escaped before Mel could pester her with more questions. Sure, she didn't have to answer, but not answering was almost worse. Once they had Mel's engagement party out of the way, she could figure this out. On her own. She loved her friends, she really did, but none of them understood. They'd not been looking. Not a single one of them understood what it felt like to want the unity of marriage for as long as she had.

Plenty of people considered her idea archaic. They didn't understand either.

She wiped the scowl off her face as Pen's little pink VW bug pulled into the driveway. Pen popped out, her pink legal pad and sparkly pen already in her hand. She lifted a hand and flicked her dark hair over her shoulder, as glamorous a move as any movie star. "You won't believe what I found today! Mel, your party is going to be *gorgeous!*"

Mel gave Darcy a look that said she would let it go for now. She hooked her arm through Pen's, and the two bounced ahead of Darcy. They knew where she hid the spare key and would let themselves into the house. In the few minutes it took Darcy to follow them inside, they were chattering away around her tiny kitchen table.

"I love the idea of using hurricane lamps, but with so many people and the drapes we're using, I'm fine with those LED lights that mimic flames." Mel pointed at something on Pen's list and tapped her free hand on her chin. "Zeke almost has the pavilion built. Do we have enough material to drape it so it looks like a tent with the flaps pulled back?"

Pen's expression of abject horror caused Darcy to clap a hand over her mouth before the laughter could escape. Darcy passed Pen a picture cut out from a magazine that showed what Mel had in mind. "It's not what you're thinking, Pen."

Breathing a sigh, Pen took the picture and smiled. "Yes. Yes, this we can do. You can't imagine what I saw in my mind when you said you wanted it to look like a circus tent."

"I didn't say circus tent." Mel made her way over to the refrigerator and pulled out a pitcher of pink lemonade. She held it up, asking a silent question with her raised eyebrows and the sloshing liquid.

Darcy and Pen nodded before Pen returned to her list. "Beth has most of the food covered. You're still okay making the ice cream?"

"Absolutely. I've been making a gallon a night for the last week. I'll have enough to make Trent and Cooper happy."

While Mel and Pen continued with their list-checking and chatter over Mel's upcoming engagement party, Darcy pulled her phone from her pocket and opened the dating app she'd signed up for last year. Darcy had fought against the urge to sign up but had eventually given in when her own methods had failed.

She scanned the recent requests, turning down over half of them within a minute. When she realized the talk around the table had stopped, she looked up. Both women stared back. Amusement, and a bit of concern, pinched their expressions.

Mel slid a glass toward Darcy. "Rejecting more potential husbands?" Her words were kind, taking the sting out of what could be an inflamed question.

"Oh, is that the dating site? Do you like it?" Pen craned her neck for a peek, but Darcy jerked the phone toward her chest to hide the screen.

For no reason whatsoever, her skin prickled and sweat broke out over her forehead. "Just checking a few things." She slid the phone back into her pocket and picked up her glass. "What else needs to be done before Saturday?"

Her hip buzzed with an incoming text. Once Pen and Mel were ensconced with planning, Darcy slid the phone out far enough to read the message from her dad. *There's someone I want you to meet. Saturday at 5. My office.*

Darcy: *Can't it wait? I'm supposed to pick up some friends and take them to Mel's engagement party.*

Dad: *Have someone else do it. This is more important.*

Darcy twisted a strand of hair and stuffed the phone beneath her leg when Mel glanced up. She would *not* miss Mel's party, but maybe she could find a way to have it both ways. One text to Nigel, and he could pick up Trent—who needed a ride since his truck was in the shop—another message via Mel to Cooper to pick up the others. Then she would be free to meet with her dad and still make it to the party.

14

Nigel pulled into the parking lot of Forever Pals, Hopper Island's pet shelter, in time to catch the scowl on Trent's face before his friend could wipe the expression away. "Trouble?" Running the animal shelter on Hopper kept Trent busy most days and often late into the night, but even Nigel had noticed the increased strain that seemed to dog Trent's step.

"Business junk. Thanks for the ride. Should have my truck back tomorrow." Trent maneuvered his face into a smile before he turned and waved at an unfamiliar blonde woman with a camera around her neck. "Night, Kara. See you next week."

"New employee?"

Trent shrugged. "Nah. New photographer for the website. She's been helping me update the pictures and bios for the animals. Helps them get adopted faster. She's really good. Shy, though. Worked with her all day and all she ever said was 'Who's next?' all day long."

"Maybe she's intimidated by you. You *are* pretty rough around the edges." Nigel chuckled at Trent's stricken expression. "Just kidding. Everyone else already gone?"

"Are you kidding? They scattered like teens on cleaning duty the instant I said scram."

Nigel clapped Trent on the shoulder and tossed a look at the squat building Trent loved like a child. "You know, you can tell your friends if something is happening. If you need help, or anything. You'd tell us, right?"

Trent gave a half-hearted shrug before moving away and slapping his hands together. "Just a bad day. Let's go! Zeke promised Mel would bring buckets of ice cream. Buckets! I could eat five gallons by myself. Especially if she makes butter pecan." His stomach gave a steady grumble, loud enough to put a starving dog to shame. Without batting an eye, Trent patted his gut in a soothing motion. "See what I mean. And Mel said six sharp. Don't be late or no ice cream." He wagged his finger in a perfect imitation of Mel.

"Yeah." Nigel shook his head at his buddy's antics. "You're wasting away over there. Any idea what an engagement party is? I mean, we all know they got engaged. Not like it's a secret."

"Nope." Trent massaged his neck before throwing open the truck door and heaving himself inside. "But I'm following orders because I'm starved. If you don't hurry up, I'll be forced to hotwire this thing and drive myself."

With a harrumph, Nigel settled in for the drive over to the Carmichaels' house. "You don't know how to hotwire a car." The lengthy pause had him shooting a glance at Trent. "Do you?"

"Long story. Needless to say, Lieutenant Johnson and I are on more familiar terms than most people know."

"Johnson? The deputy on Mimosa? This is a story I need to hear. He's barely older than us. Can't be more than, what? Thirty?"

Trent let the silence continue so long, Nigel began to assume the story was either painful or embarrassing. He kept his mouth shut, knowing he'd have no chance of learning the truth if he pushed Trent. The man could make a clam proud with his ability to keep his lips zipped. Something Nigel had appreciated on many occasions but found himself annoyed with when they were a mile away from their destination and Trent still sat like a knot on a log.

Trent shifted in his seat, a low chuckle breaking Nigel's concentration. "Fine. That summer after graduation, I did something stupid."

Nigel's shoulders hunched. He remembered that summer too well. But not for the same reasons. Couldn't be. "Look, you don't have to tell me."

"Oh, don't go all feminine and reverse psychology on me now. It's no real secret, and Johnson got over it years ago. I broke into his house. His dad's house back then. The lieutenant was a new deputy, fresh from the academy." Trent raked a hand through his hair, standing it on end like some sort of wild man. "His old man refused to press charges, and I spent my summer hauling manure from the ranch down to Fairhaven for fertilizer. Johnson made some kind of deal with Melbourne from Switchback and Samuel at the landscaping place. Best worst summer of my life."

"Sorry, man. I never knew."

"Yeah, well—" Trent shrugged and shifted again. "You had your own thing going that summer. Now, if you don't mind, I'd like to pretend this conversation never happened."

"Yeah, yeah." Nigel waved a hand before flicking on the blinker and turning into Mel's parents' driveway. "Still don't know what we're doing here."

The intrusive conversation left in the truck, Nigel and Trent shoved each other up the walk, each one laughing louder than the last. Mel opened the door before Nigel could rap his knuckles on the frame, and the smile lighting up her face could brighten even the gloomiest day.

"You're here!" Mel took them each by a hand and pulled

them through the house. They tromped straight to the back door and out onto the back deck.

"You know, you could have told us to meet you around back." Nigel rubbed the fingers of his free hand together, attempting to remove the tingle that shot through his extremities at the sight of Darcy across the yard. A man he didn't recognize had an arm over her shoulders, his posture relaxed and sure, as though he had the right to be so familiar. Nigel threw a look at Mel, who gave an apologetic crinkle with her nose that said she had no idea.

She reached for a cup and passed him what looked like fruit punch.

"You sure it's safe to drink the Kool-Aid?" He grinned and pointed at the rows of tables about to break beneath the weight of food. "Some party."

Mel blushed a vivid shade of pink and brushed her knuckles together, causing her ring to bounce a rainbow of light from the lanterns. "Thanks."

Just then, Darcy looked up from the cup in her hand and caught Mel's eye. She lifted her glass as though in toast, and Mel blushed again. Darcy smiled and tucked herself under the stranger's arm.

Nigel pulled his hand down his face, drawing his mouth into a scowl. He couldn't bring himself to confront Darcy. There was no need, anyway. He had no right to her. Their week together at camp—a week he'd thought might be pushing them forward—had obviously been just another week. "I'm guessing Pen put all this together?"

It was her style. From the sheer curtains billowing in the gentle breeze to the hurricane lanterns flickering with a romantic glow, the scene oozed sophistication with a touch of whimsy.

Darcy's laugh cut through the chatter of multiple friends. The sound brought him around on his heel. He should go. Get out of here before he did something he would regret. Mel would understand. The brief flash he'd seen cross her face was enough to tell him she knew he struggled.

Before he could take a step, Darcy turned his way, grabbed her date by the arm, and pulled him across the grassy lawn. Nigel stifled a groan and locked his jaw into what he hoped was a congenial expression. He feared it looked more like a grim reaper than a friend, but under this amount of pressure, he was lucky nothing worse seeped out.

"There you are. I was afraid you weren't coming." Darcy hauled the man to her side and gave him an adoring look that made Nigel force a growl down. "This is Charles. He runs a software company in Charlestown."

"Convenient." It took all his strength to keep his arms by his sides and the sarcasm low enough that the confused expression on old Charlie's face barely shifted.

Darcy, on the other hand, caught the implication and covered it with a throaty chuckle. "Oh, Charles has heard all the jokes already. I thought Zeke would never run out of one-liners. I can't remember half of them." She patted Charles' hand where it rested on her shoulder.

The urge to ask why the man thought he had the right to touch Darcy died as swiftly as a goldfish on land. He had no right. Neither of them. But this sad sap with his hooked nose and hair sticking out like a badly baled roll of hay could scram. Darcy deserved better than the two of them together. Nigel clamped his hands together and locked them behind his back. "Nice to meet you. I have to go. See you later, Darcy."

Stiff-backed and with a glare that parted company like Moses' staff did the Red Sea, Nigel cut straight to Mel and Zeke where he offered his apologies and his congratulations.

Mel hiked an eyebrow at him, but he merely shook his head.

"You really should tell her." Mel squeezed Zeke's hand, and

the love in her eyes squashed what little bit of restraint Nigel had left.

His tone grated deep enough to reach the ocean floor. "Even if I wanted to, she'd never want me." After hearing Darcy talk for years about the type of man she wanted—a man so different from him it was laughable—he knew better than to hope. It would take a God-sized change of expectations for Darcy to see him...really see him. And based on his reactions just now, his own feelings were only growing stronger. How bad would it be when she announced her own engagement? When the church doors opened to reveal Darcy in a wedding dress walking toward a man who wasn't him?

If a heart could stop and the person stay alive, that was the feeling pummeling his chest. Aching loss. Excruciating pain of something he'd never had but was still forced to mourn. If he could control his heart, he would ensure this torment never returned. Sweat broke over his face, and he swiped it away with an apology to the happy couple. "I can't do this. I'm sorry. I had no idea it would be like this. Don't let me ruin your night."

Mel chewed her cheek and leaned against Zeke, who slapped Nigel's back, effectively knocking some sense back into him. He choked down his bitterness and tried a smile. He could be happy for his friends. He *would* force himself not to ruin their occasion. "I'm okay. Go. Mingle. Announce. Do what you're supposed to do. I'm fine." *God, please make it so.*

"Why don't you go see Cooper? He's hiding somewhere around the swing where the ice cream is." Mel squeezed Zeke's hand and started pulling him toward an octagon-shaped platform. Each pillar had been draped in swaths of white, tied against the wood with silver bows shot through with streaks of royal purple. The material draped overhead, creating a tent canopy that sheltered those inside against the afternoon glare. Music began to linger in the air, soft strains of something he knew but couldn't place. Zeke took Mel into his arms and began a slow dance around the perimeter.

Backing away from the sight, Nigel searched for the area Mel had pointed out. No doubt, that's where he'd find Trent, as well as Cooper. Mel's brother had nearly as many bad dates as Darcy lately. Heaven forbid the two of them decide to date each other. Nigel snorted, then quickly ducked his head when several people turned in his direction. He'd best move away from the happy partiers before he ruined everything. Before someone took his annoyance for jealousy toward Mel and Zeke and new questions peppered him into revealing the true cause of his distress. Or worse, someone decided to start a rumor he'd been seen pining over Mel at her engagement party.

15

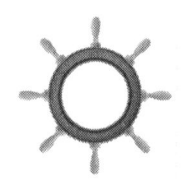

Long after the party ended, Darcy moved around the yard, picking up empty cups and moving food into the house. Mel, Zeke, Pen, Nigel, she lost count of all the people coming and going around her. They all helped clean up the effects of a successful engagement party. Darcy smiled at Mallory as she breezed by, her arms filled with fabric from the drapery. She considered each person here a friend, and any of them would be happy to help her answer the questions Mel had stirred up a few days ago.

Her phone pressed against her hip, a tingle of anticipation ran through her. She'd promised not to check her notifications until after the party. Now that things had slowed, the desire to see if anyone else had requested a date made her palms itch. The sudden need coursing through her curled her fingers into fists.

Had she become addicted to the site? Darcy halted mid-step, her mouth falling slack. How often did she check her notifications, ten times a day? Twenty? Every time she had a down moment, seeing those little hearts gave her a boost of confidence and a rush of belonging. Dropping onto the stoop, she pulled the phone from her pocket, opened the site, and deleted her account. She couldn't take time to think about it; otherwise, she knew she'd find a way to convince herself it was all normal.

Mel lowered herself onto the step and patted her knees. "That was fun." She reached over to loop her arm through Darcy's. "I hope it wasn't too upsetting for you, Darcy."

Shaking herself out of the blanket of fog, Darcy bumped Mel with her elbow. "I'm happy for you two. This party, your engagement, has been the highlight of my summer. Nothing about you being happy would ever make me sad. I had a startling revelation while sitting here."

"Glad to hear it. Now, tell me about this revelation. Sounds heavy."

"I should probably finish helping." Darcy moved to stand, but Mel held her fast.

"We're done for tonight. Everyone's gone home. Just you and me now. Mom and Dad are headed to bed, so we have all the time in the world."

Darcy tapped her fingers over the blank phone screen and sighed. "I feel like a broken record. All we ever talk about is me and how I'm still looking for a husband. Let's talk about something else. Where are you going for your honeymoon? What do we need to plan first for the wedding? It's in six months. That's not much time."

Mel's eyes went dreamy in the porch light. All thoughts of troubles slipped away with the anticipation of wedded bliss. As she drifted into a land of white satin and cotton candy clouds, Darcy leaned back, her weight resting on her elbows, and let herself imagine the vision Mel created. She wanted to incorporate Daphne, of course, since the hound's escape had led to her and Zeke spending so much time together.

Hours later, tucked beneath the soft weight of an heirloom blanket, Darcy scanned the list of names she'd created based on the dates she'd accepted, and rejected, from the island dating site over the past year. She had kept herself off the site, but the email notifications hadn't been hard to find. One hundred names. Bile rose with each comment she wrote on *why* she had decided each man was not right for her.

Peter Conrad: spent the date talking about feet. Brandon Fletcher: wanted a list of all previous ex boyfriends so he could look them up and compare. Donovan Tate: apologized at least once every ten minutes. Sean Daniels: asked for a picture he could use in his lingerie magazine. Darcy squinted at that one. Okay, so likely a legitimate concern there. The others, though? She pressed the pencil eraser into her forehead and ran her fingers along the metal spirals holding the notebook together.

Unwillingly, her gaze shifted to the list of men she'd rejected without a date. The reasons listed covered everything from "lived too far away" to "shifty-looking eyes". Darcy closed her own eyes and groaned. This was what her life had been reduced to? Trying to pick a man from a lineup?

Conviction burned from tip to toe. Where did things go so wrong? She walked herself through the last few years, and each decision that had brought her to the point where she was deciding against meeting someone because he had a chipped front tooth. *Really! You said no because of a tooth? When did you become so shallow that every flaw became insurmountable? What even made it a flaw in the first place? That whole "you have a great personality" being a cover for someone who was less than perfect physically wasn't what you were supposed to become. No more.*

Throwing herself against the pillows, she pulled the quilt over her head and spent her night tossing and turning.

The next morning, Darcy grunted and strained backward, trying to haul the massive bucket of flowering beauty toward the hole she'd spent all morning digging. "Should have dug...the hole...by the stupid plant." She exhaled and tried again. Her gloved hands slid off the slick, black plastic and tossed her on her backside. Throwing her hands into the air, Darcy fell onto her back and crossed her wrists over her eyes.

Her lungs burned, fingers ached, and legs trembled. Working a pirate tour boat and riding horses still hadn't prepared her for the strain of moving fifty-pound trees all morning. The first had been a cinch. The second and third a chore. This fourth one might be her limit. And she had four more after this one. "What did I get myself into?"

Not expecting an answer, the deep masculine "Need help?" caused her to jolt as though she'd handled a live wire.

"Nigel? What are you doing out here?"

"Well, after the third banshee scream, I thought maybe I should check on you." Leash wrapped in one hand, Nigel waved the other toward her row of leaning Hibiscus trees. "Tree fairy drop by?"

"More like the Sam fairy." Inching her way upright, she twisted side to side in an attempt to loosen the muscles tightening with every moment.

Incredulous, Nigel dropped to one knee and unclipped Shep from the leash. "She just dropped them off? That doesn't sound like Sam."

"I asked her to. I wanted to do this myself." She reached for the bucket, digging a small trench in the sand as she pulled it toward her legs. "How hard can it be to plant eight trees?"

"Considering you're digging holes by hand instead of using Sam's machine, I'd say pretty difficult." Shaking his head, he reached for the bucket and lifted it without even straining.

Massaging her tired muscles, she glared at Nigel. "I sort of hate you right now."

"Aw, you say the nicest things."

Before she could convince her legs to carry her, Nigel had removed the tree, dropped it into the hole, and had it halfway covered. He continued working while Shep danced around him, snapping at clods of dirt and sand as they sprayed the air.

If it wasn't for the tired lines around his eyes and the way he avoided her gaze, she would have sworn his attitude at Mel's party Friday night had been a figment of her imagination. "What did you think of Charles?" Taking the bull by the horns often proved the best way to deal with Nigel...and her own issues.

His grunt was less than encouraging, but he looked up and met her eyes for the first time since she'd tried to introduce him to her date. Another man she had discounted after a handful of hours when his laugh made her teeth clench.

"What did *you* think of Charles?" He spat the question with the speed of a machine gun, brushed his hands together, and moved toward the stake she'd hammered into the ground to mark where her next tree should go. He didn't ask if he could help. He didn't ask where she wanted the hole dug. He simply knew. And that knowing usually soothed her. It showed he paid attention. That he understood her in a way no one else ever had. Any other time, she would be grateful.

Not today.

"I thought he was rather dashing. He's quite accomplished. Has a massive portfolio invested in stocks with unreal returns and the pictures of his home are to die for." Darcy infused warmth and awe into her tone, daring Nigel to take the bait. For some reason, she *needed* a reaction from him. Needed justification for the disappointment she'd seen in his face when he saw her with Charles' arm around her shoulders.

What did he care? Why did he care? They'd been friends for as long as she could remember. He'd never shown any emotional reaction to her dates before. Then again...had he ever *seen* her on a date before?

Nigel tossed the shovel to the ground and stalked to the waiting tree. His jaw worked in a back-and-forth motion until he had the roots in the hole and the shovel back in his hands. "I have one question." He lifted his head, and his gaze bored into hers, sending a shiver down her spine. Raw anger burned with each word. "Are you in the habit of letting strange men put their hands all over you?"

"I don't see how that's any of your business." Her arms crossed over her chest before she could stop the movement.

Nigel matched her posture, gray eyes bleaker than hurricane clouds. "You're right. It's not my business. I'm just your friend. And I'm a guy who knows what it looks like when a woman you've just met lets you act like you're already in a relationship. I'd bet a week's salary he tried to kiss you last night." When she flattened her lips and hugged her elbows to her stomach, Nigel shoved both hands through his hair, leaving streaks of sand. "You're naturally affectionate, Darcy. That's not your fault. It's one of the things I love about you, but it also worries me. Men think differently from women."

"You're saying I might as well walk around with a sign around my neck that says I'm easy pickings." She scrunched her nose and laughed. "He did try to kiss me, though. Even after I told him we were wrong for each other."

"It's not funny. Pair that with a man who won't take no for an answer..." Nigel snapped his head around, breaking eye contact. "Just be careful. There's no telling what I'd do if you were ever hurt."

Leaving her in shock, Nigel planted the remaining trees before whistling for Shep and returning to his cottage without another word. She came close to chasing after him, demanding he explain. Before she could, his truck engine roared. Right. Saturday. Nigel worked today, and she didn't. Following him to the ship would be pointless.

An ambush at church? Her chin dropped to her chest in an exhale. Was she chasing him for an explanation...or something else? He'd left her feeling dissatisfied with the conversation and her nerves alive with an unusual tension. Because for the first time, he'd shown a piece of his heart. And now she wanted more.

16

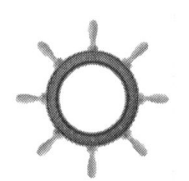

The next week without seeing Nigel rubbed Darcy raw as sand in her bathing suit.

Standing on the *Treasure*'s deck, legs wide to compensate for the rocking ship, the anger still hadn't left his proud face.

They worked through the morning, giving the appropriate nods and smiles, but inside, something shifted. Every time his gaze dropped to hers, a tingle shot through her stomach, giving it a crawly feeling like caterpillars had been let loose inside. She couldn't concentrate, nearly falling from the rigging when her hand missed the rope trailing from the crow's nest.

Captain Black delegated her to deck duty after that little mishap. Even though she was the best climber. Her distraction couldn't come at the show's expense.

Nigel continued to scowl, an expression fitting his character and drawing oohs and ahhs from the crowd as he crossed swords with another pirate. They danced around the deck, the clang of metal ringing sharp.

Bernie landed beside Darcy, his bill open in a squawk as Captain Black took them back to shore. After the passengers departed, their elderly captain turned to Darcy. "Mind the cabin for me, Darcy, while I check on my family. They're coming in from the mainland today. I'm supposed to meet the ferry, but I'll be back in time for the next tour. Keep the next batch of guests entertained. You know the drill."

"Aye, aye, Captain." Darcy grinned and patted her weapons. "Anything for the meanest pirate across the seas."

"You hush now." Captain Black guffawed and pointed toward the cabin. "Go on inside. There are drinks in the cooler. I'll tell the others you're in charge."

Darcy retreated without argument. He was her boss, after all. Even if her father owned the tour company and every stick of wood on the *Treasure*. Once you stepped on board, Captain Black was in charge.

Ensconced in the cabin with a cold lemonade in one hand and her boots on the desk, she relaxed and closed her eyes. Images of Nigel danced with each bump of the ship's hull. The shouts of crew members filled the air, announcing the passengers' arrival, followed by the rumble of feet as everyone scurried across the deck.

Angry voices shot through the air, drawing Darcy from the Captain's cabin and out onto the deck. Since the *Treasure* remained docked until Captain's return, Darcy had enjoyed her brief reprieve from the sweltering sun. The source of anger came into focus and pulled a gasp from her lungs.

Nigel faced off against a man at least head and shoulders taller and a hundred pounds heavier. No lightweight himself, Nigel still looked on the edge of scrawny when put against such brawn.

"I'm tellin' you, I want my money back, and I want it back now." A deep frown carved trenches across the man's face, and he balled his hands into fists big enough to crush Nigel's head.

Holding up a palm, Nigel tried to sooth the irate man. "I'm sorry, sir, but this boat has a no refund policy. There's nothing I can do. We don't keep money on the boat. I couldn't help you, even if there *was* a refund policy."

Red suffused an already ruddy complexion, and the man bellowed. "I'll have my money, one way or the other!"

"What's going on?" Darcy clomped down the four steps and landed on deck behind Nigel.

Without turning around, Nigel gave a careless wave. "I have it under control, Darcy. Just someone having trouble understanding the *Treasure*'s policies."

Her father's policies, he implied with the dark tone of voice. Something he would not admit here. Not with this man looking for a fight. She couldn't deny the rush of gratitude that kept this man from knowing her father was the one responsible for his money problem. She took another look at the man swaying drunkenly, recognizing the red eyes and stumbling steps as an all too familiar problem they often dealt with on Mimosa. With so many casinos and bars, many customers got soused then thought a pirate tour would be a grand idea. Most never read the brochure, or the signs posted all around the ticket booth along the deck, giving notice that the *Treasure* was a Christian-themed pirate tour.

This drunk, she wouldn't call him a fool but the urge tickled her tongue, undoubtedly had taken offense to their songs or something else in the storytelling. The rough-and-tumble atmosphere of a true pirate ship was in the opposite direction to their goals.

"Nigel's quite right, sir. I'll ask you to disembark from the *Treasure* and continue your vacation elsewhere. Perhaps The Tipsy Diver would be more to your liking." She referenced the nearest casino and watched in fascination as his complexion darkened to an unhealthy shade of maroon.

"Why you little—" He rushed toward her, arms preceding him like an overwrought octopus.

Stepping to the side, Nigel used the man's momentum to

shove him toward the deck. Staggering, the man continued barreling toward Darcy instead of falling. He looked quite amazing, actually, lumbering toward her, growing larger with each second. Nigel shouted something at her, waving his arms while trying to get ahead of the tumbling man.

He slammed into her with an impact she imagined football players dealt with on a daily basis. With his overwhelming size difference, she didn't stand a chance against the crushing blow. She moved entirely against her will, her body slicing across the deck. Her back pressed to the rail for a mere second before she was sent tumbling into the chill ocean waters.

Cold saltwater closed over her head before she had a chance to gulp a lungful of air. She kicked her legs and willed her arms to propel her back to the surface. Her pirate costume hampered every move, and its sodden weight threatened to drag her into the depths. A laugh threatened to bubble up, a moment of panic popping the idea of descending into Davy Jones's locker as hilarious.

Somewhere nearby, a muffled thump washed through the water, and her hand brushed barnacles. She cringed, wishing she could wipe away the feel of the crustaceans that lined the bottom of every boat in the harbor.

A shout, followed by a heavy splash, rocked her against the ship's hull, scraping her arm against a barnacle. Sharp pain begged her to gasp, and only knowing she'd drown kept the noise inside her throat. Murky, green water surrounded her, and she flailed her arms, pushing away from the boat.

She shuddered when something moved through her hair, but then it gripped tight and gave a yank. Before she could scream, Nigel's face came into view. He reached for her arm, pulling her close, then gave a tug on the rope around his waist. Together, they shot toward the surface.

Breaking from water to blessed air, she could have cried in relief, but managed to hold back the tears and breathed in great gulps of briny air that tasted like raw fish. Nigel pushed her ahead of him, her back against his chest, and placed her hand on the rope ladder.

"You first. I'll be right behind you in case you need me." The raw panic and gravelly tone encouraged her to accept the offered help without argument.

As they ascended, Nigel stayed no further away than a single ladder rung. The rope remained around his waist in case they took another tumble into the ocean. But Darcy knew Nigel would never let her fall.

Captain Black met them at the rail, helping to haul Darcy over first before his expression pained and he grasped Nigel's hand. "Well done, son. You two get changed and dried off. You're sitting out this trip. We'll pick you up for the next one."

Nigel nodded, still breathing hard. He untied the rope and tossed it toward the remaining crew members before taking her by the elbow and leading her toward shore.

"I think I can walk without your help." Darcy tried for a light tone, but Nigel's scowl said he wasn't ready to joke around just yet. "Thank you, Nigel."

"My fault you went over." Shaking his head, he sent drops of water flying in all directions. "Should have done better."

"It's not your job to protect me."

"Maybe not. But someone should." He held up a hand when she started to argue. "Not because you're not capable. Because you're worth it. You're worth worrying about. Spending sleepless nights wondering if you're okay. You're worth that."

She wanted to ask if he'd been spending sleepless nights worrying. The question hit the tip of her tongue, but the dark rings circling his eyes answered well enough. Did that mean he'd worried about *her*? *Why*?

Before she could ask, he nudged her toward the booth where they kept spare uniforms and changes of clothes for moments of "just in case". This was the first time they'd ever been needed.

She had to appreciate the foresightedness that had pushed Nigel to ask for this accommodation the first year he began the tours. It had been a battle to get her dad to agree, but he'd acquiesced upon Darcy's request when she joined the fray.

Leaving the small locker room half an hour later, Nigel waited for her, arms crossed and yet another scowl squinting his eyes. "I'll walk you back."

"You're not working?"

"Cap just called. I'm needed at the office." A puff of air blew out his cheeks, and he swiped a hand over his sweating forehead.

Nervous? Or simply melting in the sweltering sun after waiting on her for who knows how long? "Dad's office? Why?"

"I'll give you three guesses, but you're only gonna need one."

"That rotten man. He called and complained, didn't he? I'll go with you. Dad should hear both sides of the story."

"I need you to take my role in the skit. We're running a short crew today. Cap'n can't afford two more missing pirates." Nigel wove through the crowd, one hand on the small of her back and the other resting on his sword hilt to keep it from banging into people. From the expressions on the many faces they passed, the vacationers misread the grip as a threat. Yet, no one tried to stop them.

Nigel asked for a favor. The sheer magnitude of that realization left her breathless. Nigel's harried pace took away her remaining oxygen.

After walking her up the gangplank, Nigel doffed his hat and bowed at the waist. "Till we meet again, mi'lady."

"It was a pleasure being rescued by you." Darcy dipped her head and dropped into a curtsy that would make her mother proud.

With a grin and a wave, Nigel bounded back to the dock and disappeared into the crowd.

17

Shoving his tricorn behind his back, Nigel knocked on Mr. Riggins' door with three quick raps.

"Come in." The gruff voice sent Nigel's shoulders snapping back while he twisted the knob and entered the dragon's lair. Dark walnut paneling dropped the atmosphere to tomb-like while a broad desk separated Nigel from the imposing figure standing facing the window with his back to the room and hands locked behind his back. He didn't bother turning around, but his clasped hands tightened. "I understand you instigated a brawl with a customer."

"Not exactly—"

"I'm not interested in excuses, or explanations, for that matter. I tire of these games, Nigel. I want you out of my daughter's life. I'm willing to up my offer." With a jerk of his head, he motioned toward the desk. "You'll be captain of the ship, receive a significant increase in pay, and an apartment will be provided for you."

He'd made the offer before—even thrown in money for a wedding—many years ago. Back then, Nigel had been young enough, and foolish enough, to consider taking it. But everything changed, leaving Nigel caught in Mr. Riggins' net. No more.

"No." Nigel clasped his hands in a perfect copy of Mr. Riggins and clenched his fingers together, hiding their tension in the hat. There was no need for Darcy's father to explain further. He wanted Nigel gone. Out of his daughter's life. For good. "I won't be bribed out of existence. I belong here just as much as you. Maybe even more, and I won't be bought off."

Anger rolled in waves, undulating with every shift of muscle as Mr. Riggins turned around. "That's enough."

"It must be terrible, the guilt you've carried all these years. Does it strangle you every time you look at me? Do you wish you'd chosen differently? Does that night play in your head, over and over? Because it does in mine. I asked for one thing from you. One thing in my entire life, and you rejected me."

"You wanted me to bring my daughter to some party so you could ply her with alcohol and satisfy your lust." Mr. Riggins slammed his palms onto the desk, anger mottling his neck.

"No." Nigel leaned forward, putting them nose to nose. "I called you because I went to a party that I thought was safe, and someone slipped me a spiked drink. I called you, because you said if we ever found ourselves in trouble, you'd come."

"I've heard quite enough."

"You've not heard nearly enough. You left me there. A scared, drugged, teenager who had no one else. I still don't remember what happened that night. All I have are the memories of what people claimed happened and waking up next to someone I'd never met. But you already know all that. I told you when I called that something was wrong. You brushed it off. Told me to enjoy myself. That it was all part of growing up."

Mr. Riggins reared back. "I've been pleasant so far, but my patience is wearing thin. This stunt today proves you can't be trusted. If not for me, you would be without a job. A place to live. You'd have nothing." Eyes sparking a challenge, Mr. Riggins crossed his arms and leaned forward.

"That's where you're wrong." Refusing to be cowed, Nigel once again matched his boss's posture. He might blame himself for Darcy going overboard, but he'd paid his due. He'd rescued her and kept her safe. "I have everything I need in spite of you."

With a large vein pulsing in his forehead, Mr. Riggins strode forward. "Explain. Tell me what you could possibly have that cannot be taken from you."

"God." Nigel lifted one shoulder as though his heart hadn't increased in tempo until he feared it might explode. "God owns my life. He chooses what happens to me. You might say the words, but He's pulling the strings. Nothing happens to me except through Him. You can fire me. You can obliterate my lease and kick me out. I've no family to help me. But you have absolutely no power over my life. I've let you stand behind the curtain, a wizard thinking he's in control. But you've never known that you're powerless."

"Well, how about this? You're fired. What do you think about that? Pack up your bags. You have until tomorrow to get out of the cottage." His arms twitched, and the vein bulged to earthworm size.

Nigel dropped his hands and smiled just enough to show his teeth. "I say, thank God. I'll be out of your way now."

"I expect you to leave my daughter alone. If I so much as see you within a mile of her, I'll make sure she knows everything." His face twisted into something bordering hatred, eyes darkening and mouth snapping like a rabid dog.

"It's time she knew the truth. But I'll be telling her myself." Nigel's phone was in his hand, pressing Darcy's number, before her father could lower his arms. Turning his back and leaving the office, Nigel shot off a text asking Darcy to meet him after work. They wouldn't have a chance to talk on the ship. Not with so many listening ears.

Mr. Riggins might call her. But to tell Darcy would be to expose his own betrayal of his darling girl. Unlikely he would want to diminish himself. Darcy adored him. Nigel's shoulders dropped as he emerged into brilliant sunshine and lung-sapping humidity. He couldn't tell her everything. His part, yes. But he'd not be the one to destroy her father's perfect image. She would have enough to deal with listening to his own fall from grace.

"Thank you, God, for Your forgiveness. I'm not asking You to make her understand, or to help her forgive me. All I ask is for her to have peace." Telling your best friend the most terrible thing in your life was supposed to be hard. Admitting you'd done wrong? Nigel shook his head. "Give me strength."

Weights shackled his feet, slowing every step toward the ferry. He'd have to stop and turn in his uniform before going home. Home. He choked on a laugh. *Now what? Part of what he said was true. He could keep me from working on Elnora. He's respected. The honorable merchant and businessman. I'm no better than a bum without his good will.*

His spirit nudged, lifting his eyes to the land. People scurried, frustration lining their faces. Children wailed and tugged on parents' hands. Overwhelmed. Exhausted. Expressions he'd seen too often on his own face. Feelings he'd gathered and held in the last few years. Abandonment. Through no one's fault save death, but a feeling he could not shake nonetheless. "…Fear not: for I have redeemed thee, I have called thee by thy name; thou art mine." The verse danced through his mind, each word landing with sincerity and purpose. Isaiah 43, verse 1. Memorized years ago at camp. With Darcy.

A shiver tapped each vertebrae, the words repeating with purpose. *Thou art mine. I am Yours. For all my words in his office, I forget the moment my mortal mind takes control. You know the desires of my heart. What am I supposed to do next?*

"And Jesus answering said unto them, 'Render to Caesar the things that are Caesar's, and to God the things that are God's.'

And they marveled at him." Matthew 12, verse 17. Another campfire favorite. But what purpose did it serve here and now?

Nigel bounced his toe against the sidewalk and spun his pirate hat around one finger. Across the street, the door to the candy shop opened, loosing a jumble of people into the already crowded streets. Several in the group laughed, heads thrown back, their voices stretching across to Nigel's ears.

"Mr. Nigel!" Young exuberance screamed like a rocket launch in his direction, incoming from the shop to his left.

He knew that voice. CC slammed into his knees with enough force to send him back against the glass of Mr. Riggins' building. Her arms curled around his legs, latching on tighter than a crab. "Hello, CC." Looking down, he took in her bright, smiling face and felt his own spirits lift. Who could ignore the flare of youthful fun?

"CC." Her mother admonished with a hushed whisper, her cheeks blooming bright red. "I'm so sorry. The moment she saw you, it was as though she'd been launched from a bow. Nothing could hold her back."

Nigel stretched his face into a smile. One of the few genuine muscle movements he'd given this summer. "It's all right. Truly. I'm happy to see she's having a good trip. And you as well?" Nigel motioned to both parents. "How's Mimosa stacking up for vacation?"

"We saw Bernie again!" CC whooped and leaned far enough away she had to relinquish hold with one hand. She swiped blonde hair from her eyes and grinned, a gap showing where there'd been a tooth at their first meeting.

"You don't say?" Nigel glanced around at the trio, noting the nods before he returned his attention to his newest accessory. "I see someone's lost a tooth while out adventuring."

CC snapped her mouth shut and scrunched her face into a scowl. Her parents grinned and shrugged. "She doesn't like for things to change. Even though she knows another tooth will come in, she's disappointed that one had to leave."

"I see." Nigel scratched at his neck and pulled the feather plume from his hat. Tickling her chin, he chuckled at her despondent face and crossed arms. He'd not noticed when she released his other leg. "Well, tell me about Bernie then. How's the old chap? I've not seen him around in a few days."

"He came to our hotel." CC's arms relaxed and her smile bloomed again. "I tried to catch him, but Mama said I can't keep him." She sniffed and swiped at her nose. "I really like him, Mr. Nigel. But Mama says sometimes, even when we love something, we have to let 'em go. How come we hafta do that? He'd be happy with me. I'd make sure he had lots to eat."

Her words came out of nowhere and sucker-punched him right in the gut. *You have to let her go. You've been holding on to her all these years, it's time to walk away and let her live the life she's always dreamed of.*

"Mr. Nigel, are you okay? You look kinda sick. You're not gonna barf, are you?" CC took a step back and twisted the hem of her shirt around and around in her fists.

Shaking his head, he handed her the feather. "No, I'm not going to be sick. You just reminded me of something very important. Something I'd forgotten." Looking at her parents, he asked, "May I give CC a hug?" When they nodded without hesitation, Nigel dropped to one knee and held out an arm. CC scooted into his embrace, her arms circling his neck. "Thank you, CC, for being my friend this summer." Her arms squeezed until his throat fought the constriction and began to pinch.

"You're welcome, Mr. Nigel." She whispered into his ear before patting his shoulders and stepping back.

Nigel held out his hand to her parents as he rose to his feet. "You have a wonderful daughter. You've been blessed."

"Perhaps someday you'll have one of your own." Her father gave Nigel's hand a hearty pump before reaching for his wife's and CC's hands. "Thank you for being so kind with CC. You'll be a great father."

His knees threatened to cave as another breath-stealing punch of regret snuck through. In another world, he might've had a daughter like CC. All he had now was regrets and a heart full of pain. *I'm giving her to You, God. Where she belongs. For years, I've prayed You would either take away my feelings or make Darcy love me. I leave it at Your feet, once and for all.*

18

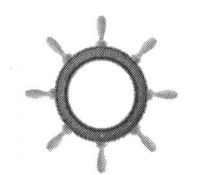

If there was one thing Darcy couldn't stand, it was women who judged Nigel because of his looks. Her conscience wiggled and poked. Hadn't she been doing the same thing all year? Nigel seemed to be the only man safe from her constant scrutiny.

The gaggle of women drooling over him as he strode up the gangplank fired her indignation. Seeing her own behaviors shot back at her...unbearable. Her hands landed on her hips with enough force to cause bruises. The women's words danced between the ditty being batted around by the male crew.

"Sign me up for the next diving lesson."

"Who knew going overboard could be so exciting."

The newest member, a young woman with long, raven hair whose name escaped Darcy, fanned herself with her tricorn hat. "Who needs firemen when you have pirates like *him* strutting around."

"Nigel doesn't strut." Scorn shot through her clamped lips. "Isn't there something you could be doing besides sitting here drooling over him?"

"Nope." Savannah reclined and thrust her chin toward Nigel.

"Just because you don't want him doesn't mean someone else won't find him attractive. Honestly, I don't see how the two of you have been friends all these years without one of you giving in. You're not...closet friends, are you?"

The implication of her words sent Darcy back a full step before she could recover. "How could you say a thing like that? Nigel and I are Christians. We take that seriously."

"Okay." Savannah threw her hands up. "Enough with the goodie goodie. Sheesh. You'd think no one around here ever had any fun. I bet Nigel knows how to have fun." She spared a glance at Darcy. "Once the right woman shows him how."

"This is a *Christian* tour boat, Savannah. While we don't prohibit fun, we do insist the crew keep certain moral standards. Not gallivanting around with crew members is one of the unspoken rules we impress upon our employees. If you want to go on a date with Nigel, do it off the clock."

"Oh, I plan on much more than that." Pink lips pursed in a kissing motion, Savannah advanced on Nigel. She grasped his hand and pressed against his side.

Nigel's gaze never wavered from its path. He'd locked in on Captain Black the moment his boots hit the deck. The more Savannah's expression pinched over his lack of attention, the more Darcy's grin threatened to break through. She coughed into her fist to cover a chuckle and turned her back on Savannah's scowl. "Well, my shift is over. Till next week, ladies." She doffed her hat and took off for land before her laughter could cause an unfortunate lesson in manners.

You simply don't try to come between a girl and her best friend. Even if that friend is of the male species. *Sheesh, Darcy. It's not like he belongs to you. You gonna insist he stay single forever just so you have someone to talk to? What happens when you get married?*

The sudden lump cutting off her ability to breathe drew her to a halt. She stopped and leaned against a streetlamp. What had previously been humidity pressing against her lungs grew into a near panic. Her breaths gasped in and out, each one coming shorter and faster than the one before. Was she standing between Nigel and his happily ever after? He'd never shown interest in any woman. What would she do when that changed? Because it would. Someday, the right woman would come along and realize what a treasure Nigel offered.

Stuffing the emotions down, Darcy straightened her spine and headed for the ferry. She needed to go home. Needed to think. Nigel's random text asking her to meet him tonight had given her a giddy feeling. Savannah's actions had soured the joy. She peppered him with text messages, asking for answers on the meeting, and received nothing in return. His silence infuriated and worried her.

Through the ferry ride and the drive down to Elnora, Darcy fretted. When she made it home, she sat in her little Mini Cooper until the stifling heat forced her out. Her cottage welcomed her home with tinkling windchimes and the scent of fresh laundry. Quickly changing from her pirate costume to a pair of ragged shorts and a tank top, she worked her way through the house with a dust rag in one hand and a can of cleaner in the other. Every surface received a thorough scrubbing.

From there, she moved to vacuuming every carpet, then sweeping and mopping all the floors. By the time she reached the bathroom where her bucket of cleaners waited, she was physically worn out, but her mind continued to tumble like the time her dryer had broken and the clothes had rolled over and over for hours before she noticed. By the time she'd figured out something was wrong and removed the clothes, they were so hot she could barely touch them. And the smell...like burned rubber. It had lingered on the clothes for weeks, even after several washes. That's how her mind felt now. It had turned and tossed itself into a frenzy of overheated detritus.

"You're being ridiculous." Slapping the damp rag against the bathroom counter, she leaned into her palms and stared into the mirror. "You've spent too much time with Mel. Now, you're talking to yourself. And don't give me that line about needing expert advice. If that were the case, I wouldn't be spending all day cleaning an already clean house instead of going outside to play in the water. That's it." She threw the rag into the hamper and stomped outside without bothering to grab her shoes.

Leaving her cottage behind, Darcy headed toward the beach. She could walk off the anxious feeling gnawing her insides while she waited on Nigel to finish his day. They'd meet up later, Nigel would tell her some crazy story, and her world would turn right side up again.

She hated this feeling of being off kilter. A ship tossed upside down, incapable of righting itself. Without Nigel to help, her horizon tipped.

Mel would tell her she was relying on the wrong person. *Only God has the power to do what you're asking. Don't put Nigel ahead of God, Darcy. He's just a man.*

Maybe so. But she could see Nigel. She could touch him, see his face light with joy when she did something right and watch his smile turn to concern when he knew her life had once again gone sideways. He never failed to fix what went wrong.

19

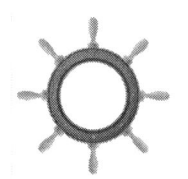

"We'll drop a sail, and tell you a tale, of a Savior who walks on water." The crews' voices mingled with the rush of waves and seagull squawks. Dressed in their usual flamboyant garb and dancing around the deck with cutlasses held high, Nigel's shipmates threw their heads back and bellowed, "He's your friend and mine, in a tale so sublime, you'll be amazed at this Potter."

Nigel walked up the gangplank and onto the deck. Captain Black stood behind the captain's wheel, arms crossed and gray beard nodding with each bob of his head. Beneath the bushy facial hair, a smile could be found, and his eyes crinkled at the corners, the skin leathery from years in the sun. Catching sight of Nigel, he dropped his arms and jerked his head toward the small cabin he used as an office.

He knew. There was no other reason for the Captain to want him in the enclosed space since he preferred to conduct all business outside whenever possible. Nigel's head lowered and his shoulders sagged. No doubt Mr. Riggins had ruined any chance of this being an amicable parting.

"I hear we've lost our Davy Jones." Captain Black settled

against the wall and crossed his arms over his ample stomach. "Care to explain?"

"How much do you know?" Dread settled like a dead weight across his shoulders. "I'm sorry, Captain."

Holding up a wide palm, Captain Black halted Nigel. "Nigel, I learned a long time ago to listen to both sides of a story before making a decision." He lowered his hand. "I've heard from Mr. Riggins. Now I want to hear from you."

Nigel scraped both hands over his face and into his hair, pulling off the dreads and dropping them onto the rough-hewn circular table. "It's time for me to move on, Captain." He shrugged away the desire to spill his guts, to unleash every hurtful and hateful thing burning in his heart. Clamping his jaw until a pain shot through his cheek, Nigel inhaled through his nose and gave a noisy exhale.

"I see." Fingers drummed against his stomach while bushy white eyebrows lifted toward the sky.

An airplane engine screamed as a jet headed toward the mainland. Nigel waited for the noise to die down before he tossed his tricorn on the table on top of his dreads, followed by his cutlasses, sash, vest, and the dozen strands of assorted necklaces. "I'll return everything else after I change. As soon as we're finished, I'll head to the locker room. Okay if I leave everything with Richie?"

Captain nodded, but the expression on his face showed his displeasure. "What is it you're not telling me? I want to help you, but I can't if you continue to shut me out like this. I might be considered your boss, but I thought after all these years, we might be friends."

"I don't know what to tell you, Captain. I'm not comfortable with this situation." No air moved in the cabin, the swampy humidity causing Nigel's lungs to burn with each breath. "I love this job. I love the people. But Mr. Riggins and I, I'm afraid we can't work together anymore."

"This have anything to do with his daughter?"

Nigel's jaw dropped open far enough for the scent of saltwater to wash over his tongue. "What do you mean?"

"I mean the fact you've been in love with Darcy Riggins since the day you heard her read the story of Jonah in first grade." A wide smile showed his joy in shocking Nigel speechless. His belly jiggled when he released a loud guffaw. "I think she's the only one on the Islands who doesn't know, my friend. You should fix that."

"So everyone keeps saying." He didn't, *couldn't*, question how the Captain knew about that. In no way was he prepared for the toxic fumes that conversation would stir up. "You're probably right." Nigel turned away, heading back into the sunshine where he could breathe without feeling like a sardine in a tin can sitting over a fire.

"If you ever change your mind, I'm sure there's other work to be had." Captain Black's voice speared the distance. "And if you ever want advice on capturing a woman's heart, I've a tale you'll never forget. After all, I did kidnap my wife and she still ended up marrying me."

Nigel's step faltered, his boot hovering above the floor long enough for the rocking ship to threaten his balance and force him against the doorframe. "Captain?"

That bellowing chuckle again. "Got yer attention, did I? You could say my crew did the kidnapping, but as Captain of the ship, the fault rested on my shoulders. Took her a few years to forgive me. Blasted woman even fell in love with me somewhere out there on the big blue." A groan and shifting of body weight followed a long sigh. "But that's a tale for another time. You've got some sorting out to do, from my reckoning."

Captain had one thing right, love was a tale for another time. Nigel's love, especially. Back ramrod straight, he marched away from the people who'd been a second family to him. He should say goodbye, let them know he'd miss them. But the idea—the finality—of saying the words forced his feet down the gangplank and toward the squat brown building they used to change into their costumes every day. If he had to anchor his boots like the roots of an old oak tree in order to stand against the gale-force winds blowing his way, so be it. Nigel Jones would not break.

He might pay his dentist a visit to fix the teeth he was sure to crack with the amount of pressure it took to hold his jaws together, but he'd not break down. Not here. Not ever.

Let it roll off, Nigel. Never let them see you sweat. They're no better than you. So long as you believe that, they can't hurt you. His dad's words rang loud and clear, even all these years later. Strong as a mountain, sheer as the cliffs below the lighthouses. Mind and body anchored in the power to withstand any storm without backing down.

That was before he knew he'd have to leave Darcy behind. Before God asked him to give up the one thing he'd always wanted. There had to be a reason. Somewhere in this mess, God had a purpose. Even if he couldn't see it. He'd rant and rave once no one was around to see him lose his cool. Until then, he'd be as immovable as granite and just as hard.

20

Something ate at Nigel. Sitting on the beach with his shoulders hunched, he looked more like a lost little boy than the pirate who'd stormed the *Treasure*'s deck earlier today. He'd looked fierce with his dreads and full costume. The look on his face had sent goosebumps up Darcy's arms.

She'd lost track of him once he entered Cap's office. The look on Captain Black's face when he saw her leaving that evening had her heart jumping. Now that she saw Nigel, thoughts fled as quickly as seagulls scattered.

Nigel was safe. He'd sustained no injuries during her rescue.

Squaring her shoulders, Darcy picked up a stick from a small mountain of sand and marched toward Nigel.

Shep bounded up from the ocean, a shaft of driftwood in his mouth. He dropped it in front of Nigel with a happy woof and waited, backside in the air, for his master to throw it again. Nigel obliged, but Darcy could see the usual joy never found its way to his face.

After Shep bounded away, Darcy tossed her stick at his feet. "I challenge you." Since the day they met, this had been their challenge. Their throwing down of the gauntlet consisted of a stick, a game, and a battle of wills.

"Not tic-tac-truth." Nigel groaned and wagged his head. "You pick the worst days to challenge me."

"Call it my gift." She settled beside him and tucked her feet into a crisscross before picking up the stick and drawing a board. "Winner's choice."

Refusal built behind his eyes for a brief moment before it blew away with another shake of his head. As she'd known it would. Nigel could never deny her anything. Something she'd known—and used against him—for as long as she could remember. She should feel ashamed, but she'd never used his graciousness for anything horrid or vile. Only to get her way, to have Nigel to herself all these years.

Guilt wormed into her consciousness. And what had that cost Nigel? Words from the crew nestled in and began demanding attention. The women loved him. Most of them swooned over the deck, saying he looked more like Captain Jack Sparrow than Davy Jones. Yet, he never paid them any attention. He was polite, helpful, and sensitive, but none of them could ever convince him to go on a date.

Darcy handed Nigel the stick. "You start."

After drawing an X in the lower right corner, he handed the stick back. Darcy went for an O in the upper left, and the game settled in with Nigel going lower middle, and Darcy cutting him off in the lower left. Nigel blocked her with an X in the middle left. She moved in for the kill with an O in the upper left. Nigel sighed when he realized he'd been manipulated into a corner. He could only block one of her two possible wins. He went for the upper middle, then tossed the stick to the ground.

Darcy completed the board, drawing her O in the middle, then dragging a diagonal line through her winning letters. This version of tic-tac-toe had a twist that usually left them laughing till their sides hurt. Not tonight. Tonight, she needed answers.

With her win came the choice to challenge Nigel to three acts of physical daring, or three personal truths.

"Why were you angry today when you came back to the *Treasure?*" One thing she'd learned over the years of playing this game, she had to word her questions with no wiggle room. Nigel had a knack for answering like he was The Mad Hatter. His answers spun in circles that came to nothing once she'd had time to dissect them.

Shep returned from his ocean rendezvous and plopped onto the sand beside Nigel, who buried his hands in the dog's damp fur. "Mel's gonna have a stroke when she sees you, Shep. You were supposed to stay clean this time."

"You're avoiding the question." Darcy poked Nigel in the ribs, grinning when he jerked away from her finger.

"Am not." His sing-song voice threatened to launch her back into their childhood. He sighed as he patted Shep. "I thought I'd lost you today. When you went over, I didn't know if I'd make it in time. I was angry because it was my fault. If I'd handled that guy better, he never would have gotten close enough to hurt you."

For one agonizing minute, Nigel held her gaze. She forgot how to breathe under the force of his despair. His eyes shuttered, closing out the emotions she'd been allowed to see. Emotions Nigel never let anyone see.

"That's not true, and you know it." Darcy reached for his hand.

His strong fingers wrapped around hers for a brief moment before he pulled away. "Next question."

"What did you and the captain talk about?"

"You're just a regular nosy Nellie today." He grinned and started drawing in the sand. Within seconds, a ship took shape. "He told me about his family. He's excited to see his grandkids. They don't visit often."

Her mouth opened to argue. There had to be more. Something in his posture, the way he still refused to look at her. He'd entered the wheelhouse angry enough to send Bernie into hiding. She was used to his repressed emotions. The way he guarded his heart against hurt, but this had been different. Almost as though he'd given up. And that wasn't the Nigel she knew.

"You should know, some flattering things were said about you today." Darcy poked her finger into Nigel's drawing, doing her best to make what looked like portholes along the ship. They ended up making the ship look like it'd been attacked by a kraken. She pulled her hand back and tucked them into the sand before she ruined the rest of Nigel's sand painting. "Several women threatened to throw themselves overboard if they knew you'd jump in to save them."

His snort showed he wasn't impressed. "Who in their right mind would put themselves in mortal danger to get a man's attention?"

"Pretty sure they were joking, Nigel."

Nigel grunted, his inner caveman rising to the surface.

Darcy imagined what he must have looked like, jumping into the water to save her. Silly or not, the picture sent a shiver of delight dancing through her mind. She'd never considered Nigel as a man before. She knew he was, of course, but he'd always just been Nigel. Her best friend and protector. Seeing him through the eyes of women looking for *more* somehow shifted her perspective.

She'd grown used to his handsome face and a body honed by years of activity and physical labor. His kindness, willingness to help, and love of God were as routine as breathing, and as obvious. No one met Nigel and walked away without knowing they'd met a genuine friend.

Nigel's head tilted in her direction, the woebegone expression slicing through her fantasy, and she couldn't help but blurt out, "Why don't you ever date anyone?"

He stood so fast Shep jumped to his feet and growled as he searched the beach for any sign of a threat. When he couldn't find the source, the dog looked up at Nigel and whined. Nigel patted Shep's head and picked up the stick for him to chase into the surf.

Threat forgotten, Shep started racing toward the water before Nigel drew his arm back for the throw.

Darcy waited, refusing to budge. The rules of the game were clear. Nigel had to answer. The breath she held confused her. *Why does his answer matter so much? I've never wondered before why he never goes out. Those women must have gotten under my skin more than I realized. He deserves someone better. Someone who loves his kind heart and won't abuse the love he hides from the world.*

Hands on his hips, Nigel angled his body away. His shoulders lifted with a heavy breath, and he seemed to hold it for several seconds before releasing an intricate whistle that brought Shep racing back. Water flew from his coat, spraying Nigel when he slid to a stop and pranced in place.

"God says I have to wait." The slash of anger cutting through the words, along with his clenched hands, showed he wasn't as okay with the idea as the declaration suggested.

"Why?" She struggled to her feet, grateful when Nigel held out a hand and lifted her up without ever meeting her eyes. The moment she felt balanced, he released her.

In his silence, island sounds surrounded her. She'd been so focused on Nigel, the sights, smells, the very taste of Elnora had disappeared. Sand shifted between her bare toes, the texture somewhere between sugar and pebbles. Soft but strong, she had to work her feet back and forth in sliding motions to bury them in the warmth and find the chill lying beneath the surface. An opposite of Nigel, who hid his warm center with a chilly outer shell.

Sunlight bounced off Nigel's hair, giving it a golden glow where the curls flipped out. He needed a trim. Reddish highlights flecked his beard, colors only brought out in these moments when he lifted his face to the sun. Eyes closed, he appeared deep in thought, and Darcy knew he wouldn't answer until he could express himself clearly.

Thunderclouds loomed on the horizon, a storm brewing far out to sea. Wind whipped up from the shore, pressing against them. Nigel stiffened but otherwise remained solid, standing his ground as though daring the weather to try and sway him.

Darcy leaned with the wind, letting it wrap around her and tease her hair into a tornado of motion. Shep chased a leaf as it spiraled down the beach, his barks breaking up the howl of the air shooting between the cottages in an eerie growl.

"We should go inside." Again, the words he spoke didn't match his posture. He didn't move. Not toward his home or toward her. He continued to brace his body against the elements. The storm would never make shore. Already, the wind was receding, and the storm clouds moved further out to sea. Purple lightning shot through the sky. Darcy held her breath, waiting for the boom of thunder that never came.

She crossed her arms, determined to stand her ground. "Why won't you answer my question?"

"You had three questions. You got three answers. I don't have to answer if I don't want to."

"Aw, come on. Stop being all strong and silent type. You're not as mysterious as you think you are."

"Yeah?" Nigel fixed a hard look in her direction. "Then why don't you tell me why I never date?"

"I think you're afraid." She poked him in the chest. "Mr. Macho doesn't want to get his heart broken, so he hides behind this façade of not caring. You're a big softie. You know it. I know it. You should let other people see that side of you more often. Savannah has been trying to get your attention all summer. One look from you would make her day."

With each word, his body stiffened until he resembled an

oak plank more than a person. "I'm not interested. I won't smile and pretend I am. She's a good person who doesn't deserve to be given the run around."

"Another woman, then? Who would make you happy?"

Nigel growled out a breath and raked both hands through his hair. "Can we talk about something other than my lack of a love life?"

"Okay. What do you think about me asking Cooper out on a date?" Game. Set. Match. Her arrows hit the target, each word sending Nigel into a tailspin of mutinous glares.

21

"What do you want from me, Darcy?" Nigel raked both hands through his hair for the second time, no doubt standing it on end. From there, he took to combing his fingers through his beard.

The lonely call of a wood stork drifted up from the shore. Darcy's shoulders lifted and anger flashed in her eyes. "I want to talk. Come on, Nigel. We've always been friends. I tell you my problems."

Nigel tucked his chin into his chest and tried to curb the desire to grasp Darcy's shoulders. He knew where that would lead. First, a hug. After that...he couldn't even think of what might happen if he gave in to one iota of the desire flooding his veins. "I can't give you dating advice. I don't even know what you're looking for in a guy. No one is ever good enough for you."

"That's not true!" Darcy reached for his hands and pulled them into a bunch beneath her chin. Her eyes pleaded with him to understand. "I want someone like you. You're funny, smart, and kind. You have a solid relationship with God. You're perfect. That's what I want."

"I'm not perfect." Nigel latched onto that phrase with the tenacity of a bulldog. Her rejection burned so deep it took a minute for the pain to set in. *Someone like you.* Not him. She would never want him.

He pulled his hands away and shoved them into his pockets. How had they gone from him being one question away from admitting his feelings...to this? "You deserve someone better than me." A dry laugh escaped. "Even if you ever did see me as husband material, I wouldn't be good enough for you."

"See you as husband material." Darcy repeated his words with a frown twisting her face into an unrecognizable expression. "What are you talking about?"

"Nothing." Nigel turned to leave. He shouldn't be here. Should have left a long time ago. Maybe on the mainland he could find some distance from Darcy. Maybe with distance he could stop loving her. "I'm taking a job on the mainland." It wasn't a lie. After the fiasco with Mr. Riggins, Nigel had put in a few calls to his friends. Zeke had exactly what he needed.

Darcy didn't take the hint, her quick steps bringing her to his side before he reached the sandy path leading through the dunes and up to the line of cottages. Lights from his own tiny home glittered, tiny flickers of hope in an otherwise desolate landscape.

He tugged his shirt before clenching his hands into fists.

Darcy bumped his arm, the movement intentional and friendly. "Talk to me. I've never seen you like this before. Where are you going? What's the job? When will you be back? Can Shep stay with me while you're gone?"

"I'm not coming back." There. He'd said it. The decision had been made and spoken into the void. No going back now.

"Not coming back?" Darcy staggered to a halt, her feet shifting sand as she rocked forward and grabbed his hand. "Stop."

Nigel kept walking. He knew what he had to do. She needed

to know the truth. Only then would she let him go. Once she knew, she'd be happy to see him leave and never come back. But he couldn't let anger overwhelm him. She deserved to know, but he could only tell this story with civil detachment.

"We need to talk. But not here." He tugged her hand but refused to turn back.

Her arm snaked around his, her warmth pressing against the gaping hole he was about to inflict on their relationship.

Once they settled around his kitchen table with cartons of ice cream, Nigel closed his eyes and pinched the bridge of his nose. "I've been keeping a secret from you."

A squeak indicated she'd heard his low tone. Her lack of immediate questions showed an unusual restraint. Nigel opened his eyes and reached for his ice cream. His stomach couldn't handle the sweet treat, but it gave his hands something to do.

"You remember that summer after graduation? You spent the summer with your parents on your dad's yacht?"

Darcy nodded and reached out to touch his hand.

Pulling his hands away, Nigel grimaced. His stomach knotted into a solid, heavy ball. *God, help her to hear this with understanding. Help me to deal with the fallout.* "I did something stupid that summer."

"You were a kid. We all did stupid stuff. Whatever it is, I'm sure it's not that bad." She reached for him again, her hand landing on his shoulder before he could back away.

Lunging to his feet, Nigel put the chair between them and strangled the bars running across the backrest with both hands. Say it. Get it out there and over with. "I went to a party on the beach. There was alcohol involved." He stopped long enough to choke down a rush of acidic bile. His throat convulsed. When Darcy started to stand, he held out a hand to stop her. "I got a girl pregnant that night."

Darcy fell back into her chair with a whoosh of breath and a thump. She squinted at him, her eyebrows pulling together.

"Explain." She pointed at the chair. "From the beginning. If you think you're going to drop a bomb like that and walk away, you don't know me at all."

"I didn't go there with the intention of doing anything wrong. The first drink was handed to me. I couldn't taste the alcohol." He lowered himself to the chair and began finger-combing his beard. "At least, that's what I still tell myself. I suspected it might be spiked, but I drank it anyway. I barely remember anything after that. I woke up beside a girl." Heat flashed up his neck as shame covered him.

He stood and began pacing. Three steps each way, but the motion helped quell the rising guilt and despair. "I woke up the next morning, and she told me what had happened." Put the millstone around his neck and hang him now. The guilt couldn't get any heavier. "Three months later, I found out she was pregnant."

"How did you find out?" Darcy remained in her seat, following his pacing with a steady gaze he couldn't meet. This question he could not answer. Under pain of losing her forever, he could not reveal her father's involvement. That Mr. Riggins had been willing to pay for everything if it meant shipping Nigel off to the mainland.

"Doesn't matter." His bare feet slapped across smooth linoleum, the chill seeping through his soles and into his heart. "She miscarried the baby."

Darcy's gasp cleaved through his heart and bundled his nerves into a knot. "Nigel, I'm so sorry."

He crossed his arms to stop their trembling. The confession had eaten away at his soul for years until he felt as empty as a conch shell. "I wasn't. I would have done right by her, had everything in place. Wedding. House on the mainland. Everything. Then, she miscarried, and I was free. We didn't love each other. She never wanted to marry me. What decent human being has even a shred of levity at the death of an innocent? I'm a monster, Darcy. A mean-spirited, deceitful—"

His throat convulsed and tears built behind his eyes as he released the years of torment into the ears of his best friend and the only woman he'd ever loved. He could never come back from the past. But one thing he could do was walk away before he hurt someone else. "So, don't look for someone like me when you look for a husband. You deserve better. You deserve the world. Don't let anyone ever tell you different, and don't settle for less. I only ask you to let God guide you to the perfect man." *And that's not me.*

Her silence bothered him more than he could admit, but it was all for the best. Turning to face her, the tears streaking down her face almost undid his resolve. Shep barreled into the room and ran straight to Nigel. Using every inch of his impressive height, the shaggy beast reared up to plant his paws on Nigel's shoulders. Doggy breath washed over Nigel in panting waves, making him grateful for the dental chews recommended by both Kendall and Mel.

After ruffling the dog's ears, he pushed Shep down. Claws scrambled as the canine struggled to find purchase and launched himself toward Darcy. Her defeated posture and the constant motion of her hands twisting the hem of her shirt lodged deep inside. "I'm sorry. For what it's worth." He cleared the lump from his throat and tried to stop the waver in his voice. "I'm going for a walk on the beach. Give you a few minutes alone. If you're not here when I come back, I'll understand."

Leaving his heart behind, he left without looking back.

22

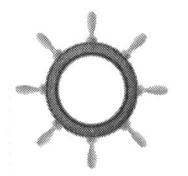

Shep sat on her feet, his heft keeping her rooted in the magnitude of Nigel's confession. How had she not known about this? Nigel kept a secret from her. For *years*. The thought refused to coalesce into reality. His deception—if she could call it that—wormed through everything she thought she'd ever known about her best friend. Why did he tell her now? When she had reached her lowest point? Darcy pushed that selfish thought away.

Her hands tangled in Shep's long coat. He whined and rested his head on her lap. It was as though he knew this was the end. Why? That was the question she could not reconcile. Why now? Why was Nigel leaving? There had to be more he wasn't saying. The constant fingers through the beard said Nigel still had a secret, or at least something on his mind. Her heart ached for Nigel's pain. Her sense of security popped like a bubble. If Nigel could betray her, what hope did she have of anyone ever being honest?

What about God? He's never lied to you. Darcy huffed and stood. She had to pull her feet from beneath Shep, and the big dog whined again. "Sorry, buddy. I need to think, and I can't do that here. I'll be back to talk to Nigel. This isn't over yet. It can't be over."

By the time she reached her own cottage, hot tears streaked down her cheeks and sobs heaved through her chest. Her best friend was leaving. Forever. If his word could be trusted. She should be happy for him, but all she could feel was sorrow for her own loss. *I want someone like you.* Her own words echoed back, mocking her with their juvenile innocence. A snort burst forth, an interruption to her snot-inducing sobs.

Sitting in one of her walnut-brown Adirondack chairs, Mel waited with her heels propped up on the railing. She stared out toward the water, her eyes crinkling with her smile. It took her less than three seconds to catch Darcy's expression, drop her feet to the floor, and shoot upright. "What on earth?" She pulled Darcy into a hug and patted her back.

Darcy tried to hold back the emotions rocketing through her heart and mind, but Mel's gentle friendship shot holes from point blank range at her willpower. She blubbered a few incoherent sentences before Mel shushed her. "We'll talk in a bit. Get this out of your system first. Just give me a nod or a shake. Is anyone injured?" When Darcy shook her head, Mel patted again. "Okay, then talking can wait."

After a gut-wrenching, snot-pouring show of blatant emotion, Darcy pulled away and lowered herself into the nearest chair.

Mel disappeared inside, only to reappear with water, Kleenex, and a blanket. She puttered around Darcy until everything was to her liking, then she sat in the chair beside Darcy and picked up a water bottle. "If you're ready, tell me what's wrong."

"It's Nigel." Her throat closed, refusing admittance to the rest.

Mel's eyebrows scrunched, and she fiddled with her water, passing the bottle from hand to hand across the white-washed, bleached-out wooden table. Something shifted in her demeanor. Slight enough it could have been easily overlooked, but Darcy honed in on her friend's discomfort. "What? You know something. Is everyone lying to me?" Her voice wailed higher than a five-year-old's temper tantrum, but she didn't care.

"What are you talking about? Aren't you happy Nigel finally told you how he feels?"

Darcy gasped for air with the strength of a whale preparing to dive. "What do you mean, how he feels? What does Nigel feel?"

"That's not what he told you." Mel's voice dipped low, the tone full of regret. She pressed her fingers into her temples. "And I was doing so well about my promise to stop assuming and jumping to conclusions. What *did* Nigel tell you?"

"I don't know if I'm supposed to say. He didn't say I couldn't. He's leaving Elnora. Going to the mainland, and he's not coming back." Darcy ran her hands through her hair, picked up the strand behind her left ear, and began twisting it around her fingers. "Just something that happened a long time ago. Now, tell me what you meant."

Mel shook her head, her hair fanning out in the breeze she created. She worried the water bottle again. "Are you upset because he's leaving...or because he's not coming back?"

"Neither." Darcy cut off a soul-searching sigh. "I've not had time to process that yet. I'm disappointed in him. Because of what he told me. But I can't talk to you about that. Not without his permission." She lifted her gaze to the water, watching the never-ending roll of waves. The crash and recoil never ceased to ease her heart. "Why would he leave me?"

"There it is." Mel leaned back in her seat and folded her hands over her stomach. "You are upset about his leaving. Care to tell me why? You've spent time without him before. You're gone for months at a time with your dad."

"He's been my best friend forever. Even longer than you."

"Let me ask you something, and I want you to think about it before you answer. Don't just spout off." Her gaze bored into Darcy. "Promise?"

Darcy nodded, her throat suddenly dry.

"If it was me leaving, instead of Nigel, would you be this upset?" She held up her hand when Darcy's mouth popped open for a vehement affirmation. "You promised to think about it. Think about what Nigel said. The opportunity he's been given. I've no doubt you would miss me, but what about this?" Mel indicated the maelstrom of tissues and Darcy's swollen eyes. "Would you be this upset if I left? I'm not trying to gauge which one of us is your favorite friend. I have a point I'm trying to make."

After a prolonged silence, Mel's voice whispered. "In all the dates you've been on, have you been looking for Mr. Right, or have you been looking for Nigel?"

I want someone like you. Her statement to Nigel would likely haunt her until the end of her days, but it was true. Mel's question swelled in the continued crash of waves. Her shoulders shook as a sledgehammer of grief slammed her heart. Nigel. She wanted to be angry with him, even felt justified in her righteous fit of rage. But what agony had he gone through? Alone. No. Not alone. God was with Nigel. Darcy could not doubt Nigel's sincerity as a Christian, but his perfect walk with Jesus was now tainted by her newfound knowledge.

"I thought he was perfect." The admission cost her a few more tears and another handful of tissues before she could hear past her own heartache.

Mel rubbed circles on Darcy's back and sighed. "I think we all want to believe in someone the way you believe in Nigel. You're disappointed in him. I don't know why, but I do know that having someone fall off the pedestal you've placed them on can hurt. Badly."

"I never put Nigel on a pedestal."

"Are you sure? Because you just said you thought he was perfect." Mel handed Darcy another tissue and continued before she could object. "We are none of us perfect. I've made mistakes. So have you. I think it's okay to be disappointed when someone fails our expectations, but I also think you must extend grace."

"I can't do this right now." Darcy shoved back from the table and threw the wad of tissues onto the table to join the cavalcade of discards. "I'm going to my parents' house for a few days. I need to think, and I can't do that with you telling me I should forgive Nigel. You don't know what he's done. Maybe I'm being immature. Maybe I'm being a bad Christian. I don't care. I need to sort this out my own way."

23

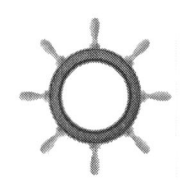

With her parents' brownstone in sight, Darcy gulped back another round of sobs and swiped her eyes. No doubt it wouldn't matter. She'd always been an ugly crier. With this hard a crying jag, her face would be splotchy and her eyes puffier than Rocky after a few rounds in the ring with Apollo.

Rolling her Mini Cooper to a stop, she sniffed and swiped a hand over her face before opening the door and climbing out. Up the brick steps and across the porch before the next bout of tears started, Darcy opened the door and stepped inside. Overhead, an ornate golden chandelier with old-fashioned yellow bulbs sent a warm glow over burnished copper and polished walnut. Her sneakers squeaked as she closed the door, and overhead, a second door closed. A muffled voice traveled from the study to her right while her mother's light tread descended the curved staircase.

"Darcy, what a lovely surprise." A gentle southern drawl with a hint of her Charlestown background swirled through the air, as refreshing as her mother's lilac scent.

The study door banged open, and her father emerged. "Darcy's here?" He held out his arms. "Darcy. So glad you're here—"

His hands landed on her shoulders and gripped tightly. "Georgia, did you know your daughter's been crying?"

"Darcy? What's wrong, dear?"

As though she'd not cried a drop, the floodgates opened once again. Through the gulps, Darcy released Nigel's name.

In the time it took for his name to leave her lips, her dad straightened with a jerk. "I knew that boy was trouble. Did he hurt you? I swear, if he's done something to you, he'll wish he'd taken my offer years ago." With his thumbs digging into her collarbones, he jerked his head. "Georgia, call the police. I won't stand by and see him unpunished again."

His words floated around Darcy like glitter in an updraft. Only these words didn't sparkle. Ashes fit this better. His words burned, ripped open the wound in her heart, and poured a bucket of lava inside. "You knew." She stepped away from his hands. "Nigel didn't hurt me. He told me he's leaving." Another step back as her father's eyes widened and his hands dropped. "You knew, and you never told me. He suddenly decides to leave after you called him to the office today. Why?"

"There's no reason for you to know." Her mother placed a gentle hand on Darcy's arm and patted.

Darcy pressed her thumbs into her eyes and groaned. "Tell me everything. What did Dad mean about Nigel taking an offer years ago?"

"I offered to send him to Charlestown to manage the *Pirate's Chest*. He turned me down. After. Well." He cleared his throat and ran two fingers under his collar. "After the wedding was canceled."

"Why? Why bribe him to go away? What threat was he to you?"

"Not me, darling. I wanted to send him away for you."

Her mother's lilac perfume wrapped around Darcy as tightly as her mother's embrace. "We're always only thinking of you, dear. How could we trust him with you after he'd proved to be so—" As she stepped back, her hands fluttered as though she swatted away a swarm of bees. "Well, it just wasn't what we wanted for you."

"You tried to take my best friend away from me." The words left her mouth but still made zero sense. "How was he a threat to me? My best friend. I trust Nigel with my life." The present tense verb wasn't lost. Even in her scattered state, she trusted Nigel.

Mel's words collided with the conversation swirling around her ears. She couldn't concentrate. Everything dipped and whirled like some kind of carnival ride. "I need to talk to Nigel." Her heart settled and the world righted itself again. None of this made sense. Nigel's actions all those years ago she could understand. Not approve but understand. He'd made a mistake. His leaving? No. Wrong. Wrong. Wrong. Every heartbeat resounded with the feeling of impending doom. "What made him decide to leave now?"

An exaggerated sigh slipped from her father's lips. "Does it matter? Good riddance, I say."

"Okay." Darcy gripped her elbows and locked her knees. "Dad. Nigel made a mistake. Yes, I'm working through it. But I still love him. I'm not perfect either." Her confession sank deep into the deepest parts of her heart. "I'm in love with Nigel."

"No." Her dad's hand sliced between them. "Absolutely not. I won't allow it."

"You honestly think you can control who I love?" The strand of hair made its way back into her hand, the twirling soothing the raw nerves. *God, it's too much. First Nigel, now Dad. Why? Why is everything I've ever believed being tested?*

Her mother wrapped an arm around his waist, and he lowered an arm to cover her shoulders. "Darling. Care to tell Darcy why you object so very much to Nigel's affections for your daughter?" Although the tone held a bit of a pout, there was a honey-smooth richness melding with the expression of calm assurance. Georgia Riggins kept her face clear of anger or distrust, her unlined cheeks showing she believed deeply in a self-care regime capable of maintaining her youthful beauty.

He puffed up his chest and opened his mouth, no doubt to object, but a quick glance at his wife's face deflated the swagger.

"You won't be persuaded otherwise?"

"She's too much like me. The more you push to tell her no, the harder she'll fight. Tell her the truth."

"Standing right here." Darcy smothered a laugh despite her annoyance. For all his bluster and pomp, Dad was wrapped around his darling wife's finger.

After squeezing her shoulder, he turned them toward the study and motioned for Darcy to follow. "If we're going to rehash this tale, we might as well be comfortable."

Her mother's hips swayed in rhythm with her husband's steps, their touching legs moving as one. Darcy could imagine her mother in an old-fashioned ballgown instead of her serviceable but lovely flowing peach skirt and billowy white top. She could be sashaying across the ballroom, capturing her beloved's eye, instead of dancing across the lacquered floors of an echoing foyer. The stuff of fairy tales and novels. And the love Darcy had craved to find for as long as she could remember.

Dual sighs and the squeal of leather followed her parents' movements as they sat down. Darcy curled into the over-sized leather recliner and pulled a fleece blanket over her lap. The urge to bombard them with questions built into a knot in her throat, but she held off the assault.

Dad smoothed one hand down his chest, as though putting his tie back in place, even though he wore a simple blue polo with the collar open. For several long seconds, the only sound came from the grandfather clock as it ticked away the seconds. A wall filled with books framed her parents' concerned faces while making them look smaller somehow. So much knowledge and history in this room. And so many things she didn't understand.

"Procrastination won't make this any easier." A poke from her mother and the lifting of her lips into a smile broke the solemn quiet.

"I don't know where to begin."

"Well, the beginning is a good place to start." She huffed and poked him again. "Darcy, darling, how much do you remember about your family history?"

"I asked for answers, and you're giving me a history test." Darcy tossed the blanket aside and moved to stand.

"Oh, posh, sit down. You act just like your father did at your age." Another poke. This time he reached across and laced their fingers together to stop the ribbing. "I'm simply trying to expedite the process. No need in telling you stories you already know. You remember your father is descended from the notorious Anne Bonny." At Darcy's nod, she smiled and leaned her head back against his black-clad shoulder. "My father knew, too, and he was not about to let his precious jewel marry a ragamuffin castoff of a pirate."

Settling back, she tucked her fist beneath her chin and widened her eyes. "It sounds like *Cinderella*. But I don't understand what this has to do with Nigel leaving."

"You're too good for him. His past is—well, it's unpleasant." Settling deeper into the couch, her father took up another tale. "Darcy, honey, you know how much I love your mother, but you don't know the troubles we went through to get where we are today. There are years of problems behind us, years of hardship, of poverty. There were times when I wished, for your mother's sake, I'd never asked her to marry me."

Reaching up to wipe away a tear, her mother then patted his chest. "And I've told him a hundred times, I'd do it all again. In a heartbeat. When you have a true love like ours, there's little that can be done to stop it. Even when it seems the entire world is bent on breaking you apart."

"I wanted to spare you that pain." Her father broke in, shaking his head. "This thing with Nigel. It's nothing more than a crush. He's leaving, so now you think yourself in love with him. Because you don't want to lose your friend. You're listening to your heart, Darcy. Listen to your head." He patted his wife's shoulder and offered a thin smile. "In matters of the heart, that seems nonsensical advice, but I challenge you to accept what I've said and let Nigel go. He deserves a chance to be the man he could be without his past hanging over him and the desire to capture your heart holding him back from his potential."

Confusion swirled in a nasty coil, tightening her stomach into writhing knots. Who could she trust? Her mother didn't contradict, even though her face pinched as though she'd sucked a lemon. Was she only thinking of Nigel because he was leaving? True, she wanted him to stay. *I've finally gotten what I wanted, and it's nothing like what I expected.*

"What changed today? Why is Nigel suddenly leaving? What did you do?"

"I believe that's enough for one night."

"No. It's nothing. You've given me nothing. Tell me the truth. You knew about Nigel getting that girl pregnant. How?"

"It doesn't matter anymore."

Darcy ran her hands over her face and pressed her fingertips against her swollen eyes. "I can't do this." She stood and brushed her hand over her face. "If you won't tell me the truth, then there's no reason for me to stay here." And she could drop by Nigel's house on her way, see if talking to him cleared up this mess. Every place she ran to, she found more problems than answers. What if she stayed in one place? Would the answers come to her?

"Let's discuss this tomorrow." Dad clutched the arm of the

couch and grimaced. "Get some rest. Settle yourself, and I'll tell you everything."

"Why don't you stay here tonight? It's late, and I'm sure you're exhausted. It'll be nice to have you home." Standing up in a smooth motion, her mother swished across the plush red rug and wrapped an arm across Darcy's shoulders. One perfectly penciled eyebrow arched. "I stocked the kitchen yesterday. How does a cup of hot chocolate and a cinnamon roll sound?"

Darcy let herself be led away. Her body held no more resistance. It couldn't take any more shock tonight. She could talk to Nigel tomorrow. He'd said he was leaving, but even he couldn't pack up overnight.

24

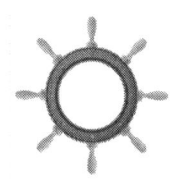

By the time Nigel had packed up the last of his clothes into a duffel bag, Shep had worn himself out running from room to room. It took only a moment to usher the dog into the truck and toss his duffel into the backseat. Everything else could stay. He could start over on the mainland. New furniture so he wouldn't have to remember seeing Darcy sitting on his cracked brown leather sofa. New housewares to block the memories of Darcy eating ice cream in his kitchen.

Nigel combed his beard and turned the ignition key. Everything ached. He wanted to pull a Darcy and curl up beneath the covers with a bucket of mint chip, but that would only prolong the pain and inevitability of loss. It was better this way. He had to believe that or risk not being able to force his body to make the left onto the bridge and drive away from the only happiness he'd ever known.

God would give him strength. That sole promise kept him as he travelled across the island and as the ferry pulled him further and further away. When he docked at the mainland and drove onto what might as well be foreign soil, a deep breath of pleasant anticipation soothed the ache in his soul. Someway, somehow, things would right themselves. With or without Darcy, his life belonged to God. And God would not leave him in this valley of drought forever. The mountain peak would come only after a long and arduous battle, but it would come.

Shep, sensing Nigel's contrasting emotions, nosed his master's hand and whined deep in his throat. "I hear ya." Nigel scratched behind the dog's ears and continued down the dark streets. He'd booked a hotel for the night and would check out his apartment at the end of a four-hour drive from the hotel to Atlanta. If things worked out, he'd have a new home by lunch and could start work the following week.

Things could have been worse. He knew that and could appreciate God's hand in the swift exit from Elnora. Not everyone could leave one job and go straight into another, especially not a job they loved like he did. Instead of working as a pirate on a ship, he'd managed to snag an interview with the IT department at Solomon Electronics…thanks to Zeke.

Nigel settled into the shabby hotel room and replayed the day at every angle. He could have done so many things differently. Would it have mattered? He drifted off to sleep, still wondering.

Just after ten the next morning, Nigel's truck rolled to a stop in front of the main office of his new home. Somewhere in the mass complex, his apartment waited. Jumping from the truck with Shep's leash in one hand and his duffel in the other, he jerked when someone called his name.

Mel and Zeke poked their heads out of the office door, Mel waving to usher him inside and out of the oppressive Atlanta heat. Mid-summer in Atlanta was a whole other beast than summer on the Islands. If he'd thought them muggy and the air heavy, his disillusion had been broken in the last few hours. Sweat had already soaked his back. Shep panted after only a few minutes outside the air-conditioned cab.

"Come sign these papers and Zeke will show you the apartment." Mel must have caught the shocked and confused expression he could feel stretching his already fatigued face. She handed him a bottle of water and patted Zeke's shoulder. "You're staying in Zeke's old apartment. His rent was paid up until this month, so when you needed a place to stay…" She shrugged one shoulder and looked over at her fiancé.

"I made a few calls and made sure there wouldn't be any problems with letting you take over my lease." Zeke handed Nigel a pen and waved toward a sheet of paper. "Sign on the dotted line and she's all yours. I think you'll like it, but if you ever need to come back home, Drew is pretty reasonable about contracts."

"I won't be going back." Nigel pressed so hard against the paper the pen nearly ripped through the flimsy sheet.

Mel frowned and looped her arm around Zeke's. "Let's go see the apartment and talk." She shook her head at Nigel before he could argue. "I'm your friend too, Nigel. Don't kick us all to the curb over whatever this is. If you don't want to explain, fine, but don't shut everyone out of your life."

Nigel followed the happy couple, grumbling the entire way. What did Mel know about what he should or shouldn't do? Sure, she was his friend. But she was also Darcy's friend. She'd take Darcy's side. Once she knew what he'd done. Terror clamped down on his limbs, dragging them into slow motion. Would he have to tell everyone the truth before they'd finally back off and leave him alone? Telling Zeke and Mel would be nowhere near as terrifying as when he'd told Darcy. He still dreaded their looks of shock and pity. Maybe even anger. He had enough anger for all of them.

If only he could go back to that night and shake some sense into his younger self. How much heartache might be spared if he could fix that one mistake? Bands of anguish wrapped around his chest.

Zeke keyed the lock while Mel grabbed Nigel's wrist and

pulled him into the apartment. White walls surrounded him, the pure color bolting through him like a physical arrow. A large, framed beach print rested over the fireplace and an oversized plush couch begged for late nights in front of the massive television mounted opposite the fireplace.

Nigel dropped his duffel with a thud. Shep whined and leaned against his legs. "It's okay." His numb lips formed the words, but even he could hear the despondent lie. "I need to be alone, Mel. I'll talk to you later." He dropped to the floor beside Shep, and the overgrown puppy crawled into his lap as though he thought himself no bigger than a dachshund.

Mel lowered herself gracefully to the floor and crossed her legs. "Afraid I can't do that." She glanced at Zeke, who had settled beside her and gave a slight nod. "I know you. You're shoving everything deep inside and trying to make everyone think you're okay. I saw Darcy last night."

He couldn't stop the jolt of shock that slammed him back against the white cabinets. His head bounced against the gray marble countertop, the thump reverberating through his skull and the room.

Zeke gave him a sympathetic wince and squeezed Mel's hand. "Darcy wouldn't tell Mel what the two of you disagreed over. Or whatever the conversation entailed. We only know that you dropped something tanker-sized on Darcy, then bolted." He shifted his legs and puffed out his cheeks. "I can't, and won't, tell you what to do. I just know from experience that running from your problems, from conflict, won't help you solve them. No matter what you decide to tell us, or what you decide to do, we both know you're going to need friends."

"Think of this as a type of intervention." Mel patted Nigel's knee before leaning against Zeke.

The simple ability to hold on to the man she loved drove the arrow deeper into Nigel's heart. "I've ruined everything. I ruined any chance I had with Darcy when I was eighteen. I thought I could handle it. Thought I could watch her live her life without me. But I can't. I had to get away. I had to tell her the truth so she would know what kind of man I am."

"You mean the kind of man who will do absolutely anything to help his friends? The type of man who would give everything he had if he thought it would make someone else's life easier? That man? Because that's the man you are. You've simply allowed yourself to forget. That's why we're here. To remind you of who you are." Mel locked eyes with him, the force of her stare daring him to believe she spoke anything other than the truth.

Nigel clamped his jaw and fired words like a machine gun sprayed bullets. "No. I mean the eighteen-year-old punk who got a girl pregnant then felt relieved when she miscarried the baby." He wanted to shock them. To force them to reel away and leave him alone. He couldn't grieve with them sitting there. The locked box rattled with the need to let its contents loose, and the building pressure forced his hand against his sternum.

Zeke merely blinked at him.

Mel didn't even bother. "That's what all this is about?" She scooted closer, not stopping until she sat toe-to-toe with him. "You're grieving the loss of innocence. I understand that. But you can't let a mistake ruin your entire future. Darcy will understand. You just need to give her time."

25

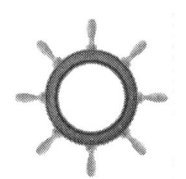

Darcy stumbled into the kitchen the next morning and collapsed onto a chair. "Okay. Tell me what happened between you and Nigel. I know about the party, and the girl. What I don't know is why you would offer him captainship on the mainland while trying to bribe him out of my life."

Her dad folded the newspaper and lowered it to the table. His sigh almost made Darcy regret pushing, but she had to know.

"Would you believe me if I said it was a foolish mistake?" Fingertips drumming on the polished oak, he glanced up long enough to catch her frown.

"Tell me the truth. Whatever it is. I deserve that after all these years of lying, even if it was lying by omission. I had a right to know."

"Nigel called me the night of the party. He begged me to come pick him up. He wasn't feeling well and feared someone had spiked his drink." Something resembling remorse clouded his eyes and his fingers clenched the paper. "I refused. Turns out, Nigel was given Rohypnol. He has no memory of that night."

"But the girl...the baby..."

"All done without Nigel's consent...or his knowledge."

Darcy flung herself up from the chair. Before she could launch into a tirade, Dad held up a shaking hand.

His voice softened. "He did a paternity test, Darcy. The baby was his, and he planned to do whatever he could to make things right, even though none of it was his fault." A heavy sigh, followed by a crinkling of paper, almost drowned out his next words. "It's mine."

"And you tried to pay him off, why? Guilt? Because it makes no sense for you to claim this was for my benefit."

Both hands wrapped around a white mug, her mother settled gracefully onto the chair opposite Darcy. "He felt dreadful, dear. The money, house, and ship were your father's way of paving the way for Nigel. An apology, of sorts. When he continued to refuse your father's gifts, things became tense."

"Did you ever even try to apologize...with words? Nigel's not the kind of guy who would hold a grudge, but if you kept making him feel like that whole night was his fault, that he had something to be ashamed of, then of course he's going to react." Mechanically, Darcy headed to the coffeepot and assembled her own cup of caffeine-filled bliss. "All these years of misplaced anger could have been dissolved with one apology."

"I've never been good at that."

"You should learn." She leaned against the counter and closed her eyes. "I need to see Nigel. I'm going home soon as I finish this coffee."

"He's already gone."

"What do you mean he's already gone? He can't be gone." Darcy clenched both hands around the coffee cup, her puffy eyes refusing to cooperate with her order to glare at her parents as they sat calmly at the kitchen table. Her stomach grumbled at the smell of blueberry muffins, but she refused to give in to temptation until she had answers. Her pulse raced as she made and discarded a dozen plans in the space of a sip of coffee and another muted stomach gurgle. The cup hit the counter with a clack.

Her father sipped his coffee before shaking out the newspaper and disappearing behind black letters she couldn't decipher from this distance. "He left his key with Lieutenant Johnson as he passed through this morning."

"I don't understand." Darcy scrunched her eyebrows and tried to massage away the bongo drums pounding across her head. "I need to talk to him. How could he leave like that?"

"Darcy, honey, maybe it's time to let it go." With another sip of coffee, he peeked over the paper and wrinkled his brows. After a long look at her face, he grunted and lowered the paper. "All right. How about a deal?"

Oh, this ought to be good. Darcy crossed her arms and waited with a scowl.

"Hear me out." He stood and held out both hands. "You say you love him. Maybe you do. Maybe you're just afraid of losing your best friend." When she opened her mouth to argue, he put his hands on her shoulders and ducked to eye level. "Give it a month. Think about this. Really think about it before you run off. I don't want you to get your heart broken. More than anything, I never wanted that for you. Don't make a mistake to pay me back for doing what I thought was right. As your father, I was trying to keep you safe."

Her throat tightened at the pain in his eyes, but the mere thought of Nigel giving up on her—on them—threatened to send her into a panic. "I can't promise, Dad." She wrapped her arms around his waist and gave a tight squeeze. "I promise I'll pray about it. And I won't leave here and go straight to the mainland to find him. That's all." She squeezed again and his arms went around her shoulders. "I love you. You did what you thought was right. You were wrong, though."

"I love you, too." He patted her back and stepped away, while taking a secretive swipe at his eyes.

With the knot in her stomach easing, Darcy swiped a muffin and her coffee and trudged up the stairs. She needed a shower, a fresh change of clothes, her Bible, and some quiet time by the water. But first...Mel. Chewing a bite of muffin and nearly sighing with ecstasy, she dug her phone from the pile of clothes at the foot of her bed and tapped Mel's name.

"Hello?" The hesitant greeting assaulted Darcy's heart. Mel knew it was her, her name and face would have appeared. Which meant Mel felt uncertain in her position of friend after their last conversation.

"I'm sorry, Mel. For everything. I was shocked, hurt, and scared. I had no right to take all that out on you." The words rushed out so fast it would be a wonder if Mel could understand half of them.

Mel's chuckle said she'd gotten the gist. "I came at you a little harsh. I'm sorry too. Where are you? Have you talked to Nigel today?"

Darcy picked crumbs off her hot pink fuzzy bathrobe and filled Mel in on the last twelve hours. By the end, she was sitting on the edge of the bed with an old picture of her and Nigel cradled in her hands. Pen had taken it one summer, years ago. They couldn't have been more than thirteen. Sitting in a tree with legs dangling, Darcy stared down at Nigel with a smile that dared him to climb up to her. And the look on his face. All these years, she'd seen it as determination. A young boy's pride that he'd not be beaten by a girl. But now? Looking at the curve of his mouth and the way his hands stretched toward her as though to catch her if she fell...Her heart tumbled.

Clutching the tarnished frame to her chest, she told Mel goodbye and fell over sideways onto her pillow. Her throat burned and tears welled in her eyes once more. *No. No more regret. No more what-ifs. Time to find answers.* She returned the frame to her dresser, then picked through her closet for something more appropriate than old college clothes. Yoga pants and an extra-long t-shirt would have to do.

Half an hour later, she settled on a beach towel with sunglasses and hat to hide the recent crying gag, snacks and drinks for body needs, and her Bible for spiritual food. Flipping through the tattered pages, she scanned highlighted passages and notes written on the margins. With no idea what exactly she searched for, she browsed with slow leisure. Her heart opened to whatever God might want—or need—to tell her, and a willingness to listen sent her onto her stomach with feet in the air.

Memories appeared with each page. Jonah—fishing with Nigel for the first time. He'd caught a two-foot shark while all she caught was a bout of seasickness. Genesis—sharing her hopes and fears with Nigel. Here, she stopped and lowered her forehead to the pages. How many times had she bemoaned her lack of romance? How many times had Nigel sat by her side and told her the time would come? He'd given everything he could to keep their friendship. And she'd never given him anything in return. Not her love. He never brought his troubles to her, but he always stayed by her side, weathering every storm.

"I've been so stupid." Wrapping her hands over the back of her neck, she moaned into the sleek pages. "What now, God? Where do I go from here?"

No words carried on the breeze. No voice spoke from above or whispered in her heart. The world continued to spin its slow dance with the universe, comfortable in God's embrace. The same place she wanted to be. Only now, a new desire lifted itself from her core and crept through her thoughts. Nigel's arms wrapped around her, his beard against her temple, and the scent of varnish around them as they slow danced across hardwood floors. It was a dream she'd not known she craved until it had been taken away from her.

Did she need a month to decide her love was true?

The sound of wings beating overhead brought Darcy's head up with a snap. Bernie landed, his widespread wings sending gusts of sand into her face. Shielding her eyes with one hand, Darcy closed the Bible with the other and rolled into a sitting position. "Bernie, what on earth are you doing here?"

A squawk answered while Bernie flapped his wings and waddled forward. When he reached the edge of the blanket, he lowered himself, tucked his bill into his chest, and closed his eyes. Of course. Sunday. No tours on the *Pirate's Treasure*. No Nigel and Shep to keep him company. And she had missed church for the first time in years.

Her heart ached with lonely bitterness before she could rein in the deep echoes of pain. *There's no need in feeling sorry for yourself. Find Nigel. Tell him how you feel.* Confusion battered against reason, dueling each other in a mad dash for freedom. Which was right? Did she love Nigel in the way he needed...in the way she'd always hoped for and dreamed of? Or was her father right and she simply could not relinquish their friendship?

How was she supposed to know? Shouldn't it be easy? The idea of not being Nigel's friend sent her head shaking with automatic denial. What about love? Marriage? Her words echoed back from months earlier. *Can you imagine waking up to your best friend's face every morning?* Mel's soft-spoken response wakened with a wild clatter.

What would it be like to wake up and have Nigel's face be the first thing she saw? A warmth blossomed in her chest and spread outward like warm sunshine after a brutal storm. Her fingers tingled with a sudden itch to hold Nigel, to run her hands over his bearded cheeks and see his gray eyes come to life. Because she'd lost herself to those eyes years ago. The first time she fell from the tree and he'd been there to catch her, she'd given her heart to the boy with a quiet soul and tempest eyes.

26

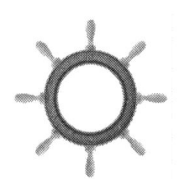

"I'll tell you the same thing I told Darcy. None of us are perfect." Mel had finally stood after staring him down for the last five minutes in total silence.

Nigel dug through his duffel bag, searching for a treat to give Shep in hopes he'd leave Nigel's lap willingly. He'd lost feeling in his legs, but his heart was taking up the slack. Instead of shocking his first houseguests, they'd taken the starch right out of him with their cool acceptance. "Why are you giving me the death stare?"

"Why shouldn't I?" Mel winged one eyebrow upward and crossed her arms. "I can't believe you've let that fester all these years. No wonder you're wound tighter than a broken jack-in-the-box. You need to let that go, Nigel. Let it all go. You've asked forgiveness, right?" She waited for his nod before continuing. "Then what's holding you back? Why the sudden rush out of town?"

"I wasn't given much choice." It had seemed true at the time when Mr. Riggins threatened Nigel with unemployment across the Islands. Darcy's dad had that power. Sitting here with Mel and Zeke, Nigel could see the cowardice in his actions. When push came to shove, he'd run away instead of standing up for himself and what he believed. "I don't have a life there anymore."

"Do you remember the story of Peter when Jesus told him to step out of the boat?" Mel leaned against the counter, tapping her finger against the marble while her engagement ring flashed in the sunlight beaming through the patio door.

What? "Yeah. The disciples were scared because of the weather. They saw Jesus walking on the water and Peter said something about if it was really Jesus, to bid Peter come. While Peter was on the water, he started to sink until Jesus pulled him up."

"Right. But why did Peter want to step out of the boat?"

What? Nigel combed his beard and thought through the story he'd heard a dozen times. Why would Peter want to leave the relative safety of the boat and step out onto the churning waters? He wasn't guaranteed to be safe either way, but why would he risk the extra danger? Pride? That didn't feel right. Peter would end up denying Jesus and ask to be crucified upside down because he did not feel worthy to die as Jesus did. "Because he wanted to be faithful." Nigel could hear the question in his voice, but the statement felt right. Peter didn't intend to do bad things. He'd wanted to do right.

"Did you know that the story of the loaves and fishes is written in Matthew, Mark, and Luke? They speak of Jesus walking on the water in Matthew and Mark, directly after Jesus fed the masses, but only Matthew mentions Peter's adventure onto the sea. In Luke, they don't even bring up Jesus walking on water. Jesus has something else to tell them then." Pulling out her phone, Mel tapped a few buttons and handed him the phone.

Her King James Bible app lay open to Luke chapter 9, starting at verse 23. Nigel read silently.

*And he said to them all, If any man will come after me, let him deny himself, and take up his cross daily, and follow me.

For whosoever will save his life shall lose it: but whosoever will lose his life for my sake, the same shall save it.

For what is a man advantaged, if he gain the whole world, and lose himself, or be cast away?

For whosoever shall be ashamed of me and of my words, of him shall the Son of man be ashamed, when he shall come in his own glory, and in his Father's, and of the holy angels.

But I tell you of a truth, there be some standing here, which shall not taste of death, till they see the kingdom of God.*

Knowledge flooded his system. He'd lost himself. Only for a moment, but sometimes, that's all it took. "Why are you really in Atlanta on a Sunday, Mel? You happen to show up here, full of wisdom and acceptance. Why?"

She stopped mid-stride and faced Zeke. "Because as soon as Darcy fled, you were all I could think about. I knew you needed us." She grinned and ruffled Shep's ears. "But we're also meeting up with Zeke's parents this afternoon."

"We'd decided to meet you here before we made the plans to join my parents for a late lunch." Zeke clapped Nigel on the shoulder and held out his hand to Mel. "Mel met them at Christmas, but it's time we tell them of our engagement."

"How are things with you and your dad, Zeke?" Nigel regretted the question as soon as it emerged. His natural curiosity had overpowered respect for Zeke to keep his private life private.

Zeke cleared his throat and scratched the back of his neck before giving Mel a smile. "Better. We're still figuring things out, but it's better."

"Glad to hear it." Nigel shoved himself upright and tossed his duffel bag over one shoulder. "Why don't the two of you head on out? I need some time to think."

Mel's phone dinged, and at a nod from both men, she pulled it from her pocket and walked to the other side of the room.

Nigel tossed his attention back and forth from Mel to the apartment. Was he really considering going back to Elnora? What would he do for work? His fingers itched to hold a pen and paper, to jot down the ideas chasing each other through his head. Anything to quell the rising anxiety.

Mel mentioned him. Her quick expression told him she spoke with Darcy. His head began to shake back and forth, warning her to keep him out of the conversation. Darcy did not need to take on his own troubles. He refused to weigh her down any more than he had already.

Mel turned her back, her hand covering her free ear as though to block out a loud noise. The action seemed laughable in the apartment's overwhelming silence. She spoke briefly into the phone before turning back. "Zeke, we should go." Holding out her arm to him, she paced toward Nigel. "Pleasant thoughts, Nigel. We'll see you soon." Her tone implied there was no other option but for him to return home. She could be right.

But he had to make that decision for himself. "Good luck with the parents." Nigel shook Zeke's hand, then gave Mel a quick side hug when she refused to let go of Zeke.

They departed together, snugged hip to hip and heads bent together. The beauty of their relationship sent him sliding back down to the floor. *Why did I have to give her up?*

If any man will come after me, let him deny himself. Nigel pulled his knees up and dangled his head over his wrists. Deny himself. An ache settled deep in his heart. He'd made a mistake the night of the party. When Mr. Riggins refused to pick him up, he could have called someone else. Walked away. No one had forced him to stay. Things had gone badly afterwards, but he'd ended up right where he wanted to be, living a good life with friends who loved him. And a best friend who he'd always hoped to marry.

Only...he never gave her the chance to choose him. He hid

his feelings from her. Hid everything from her. Only when there was no other choice did he tell her the truth and give it over to God. But he didn't give it to God. He gave Darcy a reason to hate him and then he ran, taking his guilt with him. He thought he was denying himself by leaving the island. Wasn't he? By leaving Darcy behind and making sure she could live a happy life without his interference?

Why did Peter step out of the boat?

What would drive someone to put their life in further danger?

The answer slugged him in the gut. Love. Peter loved Jesus. He trusted Jesus with his very life. Believed that even if his own faith failed, Jesus would save him.

I'm so sorry. Head pressed against his knees, Nigel let the tide of emotion wash over him. He didn't have the faith to step out of the boat. He'd clung to the mast, hoping it would save him from drowning when the only true hope rested in the One who walked on water.

27

"Let's take a ride, Bernie." Darcy pushed herself up from the blanket, gathered her items, and retreated to the house. Her parents remained in the kitchen, apparently oblivious to her trouble. She suspected the thought was unfair so shut down the train before it could leave the station. "I'm taking the jet ski over to Skye. I'll be back later."

"What? Why?" Her mother lurched upright, jostling the table and sending coffee sloshing over the rim of her cup. "What if it storms?"

Darcy eyed the perfect sky and shrugged. "Then I'll stay until the storm passes. There are still some cabins down there where I can hide out."

"Darcy."

"I'll be fine, Mom." Darcy snatched the keys from the cluttered drawer and backtracked out of the house and down to the dock. Bernie squawked and followed, waddling with each step. Pesky bird couldn't pass up a ride. He became the world's worst toddler if you tried to leave him behind. Even though he could fly himself there and back again a dozen times, he loved perching on the bow and complaining. "You're going to be disappointed. No room for you on the jet ski. You'll have to fly."

As she steered the small vessel toward the smallest of the Islands, Darcy braced against the wind and let it clear away the last of her foggy emotions. She knew what she wanted. But how to get it? Was it as simple as calling Nigel and asking him to come home? This was not a conversation she could send in a text. Or even fully acknowledge over the phone. She needed something to pull him back. A hook he couldn't resist. Like that tasty bit, every great author had the ability they used to draw in their readers. But what could draw Nigel from his self-imposed exile and back home, where he belonged? Could she pretend to capsize and need rescue? Nah. That would take too long. And had too many things that could go wrong. Plus, it would be an affront to her independence to play at being a damsel in distress. A woman in need of help was no laughing matter, but neither should it be used to their detriment.

Nigel deserved to hear her declaration face-to-face. After all his years of waiting, she wanted to see him when the words sank in. Her imagination was vivid but not perfect. Nigel deserved the perfect moment. The perfect everything.

Perfect. Perfect. Perfect. The word pulsated with a life of its own. It's what had gotten her in this mess to begin with. The need to make everything perfect. Hang it all. In her attempts to leave her family's pirate legacy behind, she'd become something much worse.

The stories circled through her head like seagulls looking for the perfect roost, dragging her thoughts away in a riptide to a watery grave. Anne Bonny, her ancestor, had lived quite the sketchy life as a pirate before finally settling down in Charlestown. Darcy's parents had grown up there before moving to the Islands when the chance of expanding the pirate tour fleet presented itself to her father.

Darcy's life of luxury stemmed from years of hard work, and she'd not been lazy in helping provide for that legacy. She had the blood of a fierce pirate flowing through her ancestry. Solving a problem as simple as luring a man back to the sea should be child's play.

Skye Island loomed ahead. Rocky cliffs battered by never-ending waves hid countless sea caves. Places her ancestors had no doubt used for their own booty during their high-seas adventures. No one had ever found any old treasure, but that didn't stop the island inhabitants from going out and searching anyway. Darcy and Nigel had crawled through every system they came across. Her dream of finding an Anne Bonny or Merriweather treasure trove drove her to distraction during her teen years. Until that summer when her family sailed the yacht to ports around the world. The summer Nigel spent agonizing over decisions of marriage and family.

Bernie squawked and pulled ahead, drawing Darcy's attention. She'd lost track of the approaching rocks, putting herself too near the dangerous landscape. Guiding the small machine, she moved to safer waters and pointed them at the short stretch of unbroken sand where most boats tethered. A small dock bounced, its moorings long ago rotted away.

She chose to pull into a natural harbor around the point, tucking the jet ski safely between two looming rocks. Her feet landed with a splash in the ankle-deep water. Shock sucked her breath away. Once again, she'd forgotten how much colder the water would be here in this protected nook that never saw sunlight.

Bernie flapped and breezed past her to land on the sand. He offered a prideful glare when she continued to splash her way toward the beach. "Yeah, well, not all of us can have wings." She pointed at the noisy bird and wagged her finger. "You coulda reminded me to wear my boat shoes."

"He does it just to annoy you. He loves to see his humans put in our place."

Nigel.

Every molecule of air disappeared from her body. Replaced with panic, she slammed a hand to her chest and yanked her gaze toward the voice.

Striding across the sand as though he'd been out for a jaunt, he approached from the opposite shore. His favorite spot for mooring his own boat. How many times had she watched him walk toward her over the years? A hundred? Ten thousand? Whatever the number, it wasn't enough. She needed to see him walking toward her every day for the rest of her life. But the expression marring his manly face would have to change. The pain etched across his eyes and sending his fingers to flutter over his beard wounded her. She had put that there. She had given him this burden of uncertainty and anguish.

"Nigel." She barely managed to breathe his name through the wind whistling through the narrow alley. "You're here."

Broad shoulders shrugged and his hand dropped as though confused. Confused that he was here? Or that she was?

"Can we talk?" *Ugh. Way to go. The three words that serve as the precursor to every break-up ever. The only thing going in your favor is that you can't break up something that hasn't even happened.* "I wanted to call you, but this deserves to be said in person."

Bury her here and now. Just leave her entombed beneath the sand with all the treasure of her ancestors.

"Look, Darcy, I didn't come back to—" He barked out a dark laugh. "Well, I don't really know why I came back. I don't know what drove me out here. I intended to go home, if I still have a home. And I found myself blowing right past Elnora. I needed to be here. I suppose it's better this way."

Bernie waddled toward Nigel, his beak open in a squawk. Darcy followed, forcing herself to put one foot in front of the other. "My dad says I need to wait a month." Her heart jolted, jerked into action by the sudden beautiful knowledge. "But I don't need a month. I've had twenty years to make up my mind. I think I've always known. I was afraid to admit it, especially to myself."

Nigel's head started shaking. "Don't." The pain built behind his eyes, turning them into a veritable storm. It built into a frenzy, turning his eyes into a maelstrom of gray.

She unleashed the power ripping through her. Love. Pure. Simple. Empowering. Her feet churned sand as she lunged into a run. Just as she'd done that night on the beach, Darcy launched herself into Nigel's arms. "I love you, Nigel. I've been looking for you all my life. It took you walking away for me to be able to admit you're the only man I've ever wanted."

Nigel caught her, as she'd known he would. He wrapped her up in his embrace, lifting her feet off the ground as his beard scraped against her cheek. "You know, I've waited years to hear you say that. But I never expected it to feel this wonderful." He lowered her feet to the warm sand and cupped her face in his hands. "I love you, Darcy Riggins. Since the day you read the story of Jonah in front of our first-grade class. I've never loved anyone else. I'm sorry for the pain I caused. And I'm sorry for the way I told you. You deserved better than that."

Darcy placed her fingertips against Nigel's lips and smiled when he pressed a kiss to the tender flesh. "I forgive you. We've all made mistakes. What matters is how we move beyond them. Can you forgive me for not thinking of your feelings all these years? I practically rubbed your nose in every date. I think I wanted to make you jealous. Force you to admit you cared for me. The more you refused, the more desperate I became. I'm sorry for being petty and childish."

"Forgiven." Nigel pulled her into his arms again and dipped his head. His lips hovered inches above hers, the storm in his eyes darkening to liquid steel. "Forgotten."

Heat. Blessed warmth and power surged at the touch of his

lips against hers. Warm and inviting, he asked instead of demanded. As though under their own power, her arms wound around his neck and her fingers dove into his wild curls.

28

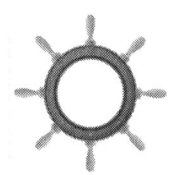

He could stay here forever. In this moment, Nigel had everything he'd ever wanted. Yet there was still one thing he needed. He pulled back from Darcy. "I need to talk to your dad."

She stiffened in his arms, her eyes going dark with worry.

A bucket of ice water couldn't have been as effective as that single look. Nigel released a tense breath and lowered his arms. "I won't stand between the two of you. We have to work this out somehow. Before this can work, I need his blessing."

"And if he won't give it?"

Nigel worked his jaw to ease the pressure before he cracked a tooth. "We pray he finds forgiveness in his heart, but I won't go against his wishes."

"You'd give me up. Just like that. Without a thought to how I feel." Darcy's arms crossed, and she rocked back on her heels. "I've finally realized I love you, and you're still going to walk away. I thought you loved me."

"It's because I love you that I won't put you in the middle. You think I'm rejecting you, but I'm trying to protect you. I just want to talk to him. Every time we've been in the same room, one of us has been angry. I'd like to change that. Now that you know about me, about what happened, there's no reason for me to be afraid of him." Taking her hands in his, Nigel brushed his thumbs over her knuckles. "I love you enough to try and make things right. I need you to trust me enough to let me try, and trust God enough to know this is what we need to do. Your dad knows how you feel now. He doesn't want to hurt you any more than I do."

"You're like two dogs trying to mark the same territory." Darcy curled her nose and grimaced. "Terrible analogy, but accurate enough. I'm not something either of you can claim as a prize."

"I respect your dad. If I was in his position, I probably would have reacted the same way. Maybe it's time I told him that instead of bucking up against everything he's ever asked of me."

"Fine, but I'm coming with you."

Nigel shook his head and pulled her into an embrace. "I need to talk to him alone first." He cut off her protest with another kiss. "Please. I'm not hiding anything from you. I feel like he should hear this straight from me, without any pressure. You can join us, just give me a head start."

"You have thirty minutes." Darcy tucked herself beneath his chin and wrapped her arms around his waist. "I'll take Bernie for a trip around Skye, then meet you back at the house."

When he started to back away, Darcy held fast, tipping her head back to give him a hard look. "I know you need to do this, and I won't stand in your way. But there's something you need to know. I choose you, Nigel. You are the man God planned for me. Anything or anyone standing in our way is only a trial we must get through."

"Then pray your father is tired of being a thorn in my flesh. Pray for us both to find forgiveness for each other." He turned on his heel while he still had the willpower and made his way around an outcropping of rock. His little speedboat bobbed in

STEALING THE FIRST MATE

the waves, begging to be released. Nigel climbed aboard, loosed the line, and let the engine roar. Minutes later, he was ripping across the waves toward the Riggins' house. Each bob of the bow into a wave sent Nigel's heart leaping into his throat. This conversation could mean the end of everything...or the beginning.

God, please, help me make things right.

As the brownstone came into view, his lungs constricted, pinching off every breath until he nearly suffocated under the pressure. Darcy's parents waited on the beach. Georgia had her hands cupped over her eyes, a smile gracing her face, while Edward stood as stiff and straight as a Navy man on the bow of his ship. Arms crossed and a deep scowl told Nigel his work would not be easy.

He took his time tying off the boat before making his way across the sand.

"Where's Darcy?" His voice cut as swift as a whiplash and he advanced. "Where's my daughter?"

"She's coming. I asked if I could speak with you alone first." Nigel pointed toward Skye. Darcy could be seen on her jet ski, bobbing in the waves. "I came to tell you I'm sorry."

"For what?" Edward Riggins rocked back enough for Nigel to know he'd shocked the man.

Nigel tucked his hands into his shorts pockets and fought to control his voice. "I love Darcy, and she loves you. I've been angry at you for too long." Nigel ducked to the side, shaking curls from his eyes. "What happened years ago is a mistake I'll never repeat. I came to say I don't blame you for how you've treated me over the years. You love your daughter."

"You expect me to believe you? What right do you have to stroll onto my property and—"

Georgia stepped between them and placed her hand on Edward's arm. "Listen to him, dear. For once, listen." He started to shrug her off, but Georgia was no wilting flower. Her nails dug into his forearm and she frowned. "You're acting the fool, Edward. And I don't suffer fools. Your daughter loves him, whether you approve or not. It would do you well to hear him out before you drive her away for good." She gave him a knowing look. "Let's not repeat our history with our own daughter."

With a harrumph, Edward crossed his arms. "Say what you've come to say."

"I respect you."

"Funny way of showing it."

Red tinged the edges of Nigel's vision at the accusation. He'd defended himself against those words spewing from this man's mouth for too many years. Anything he said about the matter would be ignored. Mr. Riggins was in no mood to listen. He only stood there because Georgia forced him. "This was a mistake." Nigel ran his hands over his face and started to back away. "You're determined to be angry with me, and I can't talk to you like this."

"Always knew you were a coward." Edward started to advance on Nigel. "Never did stand up for yourself. Always running away."

Nigel wheeled to face the man who had tormented him every moment of every day for fourteen years. "It takes more strength to walk away and do the right thing than it does to swing fists and do the devil's work."

Edward shook off Georgia's grip and clamped his hand on Nigel's arm. "I'll show you devil's work, boy."

"Edward." Georgia's voice held a hint of panic amid the layers of censure. "Edward, unhand him this instant. There's something wrong with Darcy."

Both men's heads jerked toward the water. Darcy's jet ski sat in the same place as before, no plume of water shooting out to show she moved closer to shore. A heavy, gray body rose from the water, dwarfing the machine. Georgia gasped as the whale slammed back down, sending the jet ski tumbling.

Nigel jerked from Edward's grasp and ran for his boat. He'd loosed the mooring line when Mr. Riggins reached the bow.

The older man gripped the hull with both hands. "This is your fault."

"This is not the time to argue fault." Nigel jerked the rope on board and turned for the engine. "The whales should have been done passing through here. But I'm not about to stand around and let the woman I love get tossed around." He cranked the engine as Edward climbed aboard.

Nigel gunned the throttle, shooting them away from the dock and into open water. Another whale breeched the surface, and the tail fin of yet another showed Darcy surrounded by North Atlantic right whales. Not purposefully dangerous, but their actions still put Darcy at risk. One slap of a tail fluke and she could be injured or even killed.

Edward had Nigel's binoculars pinned to his eyes. "I see her. She's still on the jet ski. Something must be wrong, or she wouldn't be sitting in the middle of the pod like that." He slapped the boat's hull. "I never should have let her take it out today."

Beneath the declaration, Nigel heard the pain and worry. This is what it meant to be a father. To worry about your child, even when there was nothing you could do to change the outcome. They would try to rescue Darcy. Only God knew if they would succeed. Every choice they made might spell disaster. But God gave freewill to all His children. That was the love Mr. Riggins was missing. The love of a faithful and just Father.

Nigel's heart ached with this new knowledge. But there was no time. They had to save Darcy. He motored them through a gap in the pod. Darcy stood on the jet ski, her arms waving. Somewhere between awe and panic, her wide eyes caught Nigel. He tried to shout as another tail fluke rose into the air. Edward pointed, and Darcy turned. As the fluke came down to slap the surface, Darcy leaped from the jet ski before it disappeared between ocean and whale.

"Take the wheel!" Nigel motioned for Mr. Riggins, who stood slack-jawed, staring at the water where Darcy had gone under. "Edward!" Never in his life had Nigel spoken the man's name aloud, and the shock of it jerked him toward Nigel. "Take the wheel. Keep the boat moving. I'll get Darcy."

"I should go." His voice pitched as uneven as the boat keel.

Nigel already stood at the edge, ready to jump. He gave Mr. Riggins a single look, and no words were needed to explain the emotion Nigel knew was stamped on his face. Nothing but death would return him to the boat without Darcy. He dove into the water, letting it close over his head and shut out all his doubts. *I choose faith. We are in Your hands.*

He would find Darcy.

29

Spinning in the torrent, Darcy tried to relax and let her body's natural ability to float send her back to the surface. She'd managed to pull in a decent breath before getting slapped underwater by the tail fluke. But she wasn't rising. Her body bobbed like a cork with no sense of direction.

Everything here was gray and murky. She could make out heavy shapes all around, but they moved constantly, never coming to focus. It had to be the whales. The saltwater stung her eyes, and her lungs began to burn for fresh air. Lifting her head, Darcy tried to find sunlight amid the grayness. A large body swam overhead, and after it passed, beams of light shot through the dark.

Darcy kicked her legs, pushing herself toward that bit of brightness. Before she could break the surface, something slammed into her stomach, pushing out the air. Her hands reached out and landed on the hard bumps and ridges of a whale's head. She tried twisting away, pushing her hands against the hard surface, but the current held her fast against the whale's snout.

Her breath gone and every effort costing too much energy

and precious resources, Darcy had no choice but to hang on for the ride. Surrender. It was the last thing she wanted to do, but the only thing that gave her a chance to survive. How often had she fought against surrender? How many times had God asked her to let something go, yet she clung to it as though it had the ability to fix her problems?

Only God had absolute power. He controlled the wind and the waves. If He could command a whale to swallow Jonah and take him to Nineveh, God could certainly command this one. Darcy relaxed her body, conserving what little oxygen remained in her lungs. *I surrender. I've demanded, and I've fought, and now I surrender it all to You.*

Her fingers found a large callus. She traced the ridges, marveling at the beauty of a creature so near extinction few people ever had the chance to see them. As her lungs screamed and her vision began to fade, the whale gave her a final push before swimming beneath her and disappearing into the depths.

Darcy waved her arms and tried to kick her legs. Her energy was as depleted as her oxygen. The weak attempts barely moved her toward the surface as the darkness crept closer. Black spots danced in front of her eyes, blinking in and out and growing larger. She continued to struggle upward…only to find herself falling.

Light gave way to the increasing depth, and her lungs gave in to their desperate need. Against her will, she tried to breathe. Water poured in, sending her arms and legs into a frenzy of movement.

Something snagged her hand, jerking her upward, toward the light. She broke the surface, gasping for air and choking on the water that had invaded her body. Great heaves expelled saltwater from her stomach, while blessed air seared her salt-scored airway. Her hands seemed to have a will of their own as they scratched and clawed at anything that might keep her afloat.

"I got you." Nigel's voice reached through the ringing in her ears. His arm wrapped across her chest and pulled her against him. "Breathe and let me do the work." He kicked his feet and paddled with one arm, pulling them slowly through the water.

Darcy tried to help by kicking her own feet, but only succeeded in kicking Nigel's legs with her heels. She muttered an apology before relaxing into his embrace. Her body had spent itself trying to stay alive. It had nothing left to give. Surrender. Tears mingled with the water dripping down her face.

Nigel's arm tightened, his hand bruising her shoulder with its grip when she heaved a sob. "You're safe now. I'm here."

Another voice joined Nigel's, this one deep and gruff. "Hand her up, son."

Her father…but…it couldn't be. He despised the open ocean. Crossing the bridges put him in a near panic. Darcy angled her head toward the glint of white slanting across the sunlight. No doubt, the face hovering over hers was none other than her dad's. She tried to reassure him. His grief-stricken face sagged as the muscles relaxed.

He gripped her arms and hauled her into the small boat. "Don't talk. You're safe. That's what matters." Helping her to a bench, he pulled the emergency blanket from the hatch and tossed it over her shoulders.

Nigel dangled his arms over the bow, his breaths loud over the sudden lack of ringing in her ears. His gaze sought hers, his muscles tense until she gave him a nod.

Dad moved toward Nigel and held out his hand. "Come on. Let's get you in here so we can go home."

Her mouth dropped open enough to allow her teeth to chatter before she clamped it closed. *What's happened? Yesterday, he could barely stand to hear Nigel's name. Now he's treating him like a son.*

As though he felt the same way, Nigel jerked his attention to the outstretched hand. He reached up slowly, testing the grip before he threw himself into the boat.

Darcy grabbed for the sides when the boat swayed dangerously and threatened to take on water. She could wrestle with this new development later. Whatever had brought about the change, she gave God the glory.

Once Nigel collapsed to the bottom of the boat, her dad turned around and settled on the bench seat beside the motor. With what looked like years of practice, he motored them back toward home. He eased them into the boathouse with more skill than even Nigel.

Before she could stand, her mother swooped in with the grace of a Southern debutante. For all her flapping hands and "Oh, mercy!" she herded them toward the house with surprising efficiency.

Nigel staggered to a halt on the threshold and glanced down at the puddle forming around his feet. He glanced up and the lost little boy expression she'd not seen in years pulled his eyes wide. Drenched hair lay in layers across his forehead, almost obscuring the expression.

"I should go." He started to move backward, stumbled, and only her dad's quick action kept Nigel from falling to the floor.

Both her parents ushered him inside, her mother *tsk*ing and insisting he put such foolish notions away. The bewildered look he sent her way tugged Darcy's heart and drew her to his side. She tucked herself against his ribs while her dad shored him up on the other.

They parted ways in the hallway off the foyer. Darcy headed to her room to change while her parents hauled Nigel toward their room with the promise they could find him something dry to change into.

Darcy offered him a sympathetic smile before her mother turned on her heel and scuttled back to Darcy's side. "I'll come with you. Let the men take care of themselves. We'll talk about everything once you're both warm and dry."

Unable to form a coherent sentence through her chattering teeth, Darcy agreed to her mother's pampering. While she stepped beneath a hot spray of shower water, her mother darted around the room, picking up sodden clothes and leaving a pile of fresh clothes on the counter. Before she closed the bathroom door, she called out, "Take all the time you need, dear. Your father and I will be in the kitchen when you're ready."

30

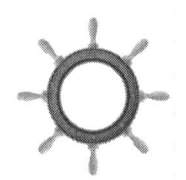

Nigel's mind whirred in fast forward as his body slowed. Without the hand wrapped around his bicep, he would have hit the floor already. Considering *who* held him up took too much effort. Mr. Riggins' face had fallen into an unreadable expression once they reached shore. His words on the ocean seemed hazy to the point Nigel wondered if he'd imagined the man's approval.

Stepping into a large bedroom, Nigel let his feet stop moving. Oversized furniture that should have swamped the room only showed its dramatic size. His gaze skipped over the mirror and his drowned rat image to land on what looked like a bathroom behind a sliding door. "Mr. Riggins, I'm sorry for what happened on the beach."

Disheveled hair waved with the force of the older man's head as it snapped upward. He'd been rummaging through the heavy oak dresser, but even his hands froze with a pair of jogging pants in one hand and a t-shirt in the other. His jaw worked open, then closed, then open again with a heavy release of breath. "So am I." He raised up and held out the clothes. "These should fit well enough. Take a shower, warm up, then meet us in the kitchen. You remember where the kitchen is?" Eyebrows furrowed, he rubbed his palms together after Nigel took the clothes.

"Yes, sir. I remember." He jerked his head toward the shower. "I'll be done in a jiffy."

"Take your time." Swiping his thumbs under both eyes, Mr. Riggins sniffed and cleared his throat. "You saved her life. She's my baby girl."

Nigel wagged his head, water dripping from the ends of his hair and showering the floor with splats.

"You can't blame me for wanting to protect her."

"No, sir." Nigel closed his eyes and swayed. His head buzzed with memories of jumping into the water, feeling it close over him, and the irrefutable pull of panic when he considered he might be too late.

"You jumped into a pod of whales to save my daughter... After everything I've done to you." Mr. Riggins' shoulders jerked up and down, and he pressed his fingers into his eyes. He shivered once, cleared his throat, then opened eyes that were still glassy under the harsh lights. "We'll talk more after you're warm and dry."

Despite the assurance he could take his time, the anxious need to see Darcy chased Nigel's heels. He showered and changed in record time, even for him. Hair still damp and eyes smarting from the dozen emotions fighting for the right to be expressed drove him from the room and down the hall. He followed the muted voices, padding on socked feet across the grand foyer and into the kitchen.

Darcy's parents sat at the table, embracing each other. Georgia cried into her husband's neck, while he smoothed her hair and rocked her side to side. Nigel's own emotions burst to the surface, and his throat tightened.

He started to step back and give them space when Darcy's voice gentled the giant clasping his throat in an iron grip. Her hand touched his back, drawing him around to face her. Puffy eyes, freshly scrubbed pink cheeks, and damp curls showed she'd rushed her own shower. He ran a fingertip over the puffy lids, swallowing hard when her lips parted and she swayed forward.

"Am I the reason you've been crying?" Even to him, his voice sounded like a truckload of gravel.

She shook her head, but her chin trembled.

He held out his arms, and she shot into them with a small cry. Nigel let his head fall until his cheek rested on the crown of curls. "I shouldn't have come back. If I'd stayed away, none of this would've happened."

A strong hand slapped Nigel's back before gripping his shirt. Another, softer hand, splayed between his shoulder blades. Scents mingled over Darcy's watermelon shampoo and the Old Spice from his own shower. Mr. Riggins' spicy cologne and his wife's warm vanilla told him before his eyes opened that her parents had entered the embrace. They circled the younger generation with a strong grip, creating a ring of protection.

Darcy tucked her head tight beneath his chin. She trembled, encouraging him to draw her tighter into his arms. The space between them shrunk to a breath, then even that disappeared when Nigel exhaled and she pressed closer.

Edward and Georgia stepped away, their sniffles speaking more than words. Mr. Riggins tucked his wife against his side and clapped Nigel's back. "I owe you more than I can ever repay." He stepped back and gave a tight nod. "I've held much against you." His hand retracted and disappeared into a pocket as he cleared his throat and cast a look at Darcy before returning to Nigel. "Can you ever forgive me?"

Unable to speak, Nigel twitched his head in a nod. As the couple walked through the door, leaving him and Darcy alone, Nigel dropped his head.

Darcy's voice, raspy from the water, brushed across the

kitchen. "I believed I would find love in a great rush. I expected to be swept off my feet in a wave of emotion by the perfect man."

"Almost drowning doesn't count?"

"Look who found his humor at the bottom of the ocean."

"It was *whale* worth the effort."

Darcy choked on a burst of laughter. When she pulled away, his heart jolted as though he'd drunk ten espressos. Her fingertips ran over his beard and into his hair. "Remember the day I jumped out of the oak tree? You caught me and spun me around. We couldn't have been more than twelve years old."

"I remember."

"That's when I felt it. That falling sensation. I spent all these years searching for something I'd found fourteen years ago."

"Only fourteen...been twenty for me. Remember the first day of school? You stood in front of Mrs. Paddleman, hands on your hips and your chin in the air, loudly declaring you already knew how to read and there was no reason for you to be stuck in the baby's corner." He tugged her against his chest and grinned when her lips puckered into an indignant pout. Giving in to the desire he'd tamped down for years upon years, Nigel pressed a sound kiss to her lips.

Coming up for air sometime later, Nigel rested his chin on her forehead. "That's when I knew."

"Knew what?" Eyes glazed and cheeks flushed, Darcy sighed and snuggled closer.

"Knew I loved you."

"Falling in love with you was like learning how to swim." She lifted her head and pressed a kiss to his cheek. "Or almost drowning in the ocean. There was this moment of pure terror, and I tried to claw my way free. In the end, there was only peaceful acceptance. An oblivious sort of revelation, and I knew you were the man I was meant to spend the rest of my life with."

"Sounds terrifying." He grinned, leaning his forehead against hers. "You have my heart, Darcy. It's always been yours. You called me a brute once, claiming I'd locked my heart away in a box. You were only partly right. I wrapped it up...and I gave it to you."

"I'm afraid I'll put too many expectations on this...on us... and mess it all up."

"I've waited over a decade for this. All I ever wanted was to steal your heart."

ABOUT THE AUTHOR

Tabitha Bouldin is a member of American Christian Fiction Writers (ACFW) and an avid reader. When she's not busy homeschooling her two boys, you'll find her buried in a book.

- facebook.com/tabithabouldinauthor
- twitter.com/tabithabouldin
- instagram.com/tabithabouldin
- goodreads.com/tabithabouldin
- pinterest.com/tabbycat38585
- bookbub.com/authors/tabitha-bouldin

ALSO BY TABITHA BOULDIN

The Trials Series
Trial by Courage
Trial by Faith
Trial by Patience

Standalone novels and novellas
Macy's Dream
Christmas in Jingle Junction
Wish Upon a Star

Independence Islands:
Mishaps Off the Mainland

BOOKS IN THE ELNORA ISLAND SERIES

Bookers on the Rocks (Book One) by Chautona Havig

Heart Pressed (Book Two) by Melissa Wardwell

Matchmaker's Best Friend (Book Three) by Kari Trumbo

The Elnora Monet (Book Four) by Rachel Skatvold

Stealing the First Mate (Book Five) by Tabitha Bouldin

Regaining Mercy (Book Six) by Carolyn Miller

REGAINING MERCY

ELNORA ISLAND BOOK SIX SNEAK PEEK

CAROLYN MILLER

1

"My word, you'd think inflation wouldn't cause prices to skyrocket like this, now would you?"

Mindy Murray offered a nod to the disgruntled customer and finished bagging his groceries, politeness—or at least a lack of nerve—keeping her answer behind her teeth. Sometimes she wondered if she had any nerve left at all, having used up most of it last year. What nerves remained were worn so thin and frail it was all she could do each day to get out of bed. Regardless, she figured saying something like "Mr. Jameson, that's precisely what inflation does" wouldn't go over too well, and as he'd always had something of a hair-trigger temper she'd learned it was better to simply put up, bag up and shut up in order to best move him along.

She offered a weak smile as he grumbled some more, paid, and walked away. Shoulders slumping, she quickly scanned Elnora's tiny grocery store, in which she was today's sole employee, and spying no-one, knowing all tasks were up to date, she slipped out her phone with its teasing urgency.

A few swipes and clicks and her heart plummeted to her sneakers. Why were people still so cruel, even after all this time?

The door opened, and Mindy glanced up from her phone to look at an older lady, whose face sagged in acknowledgement of just who was serving today. "Hello, Mrs. Hart."

"*Meez* Murray." The stiffening following the sinking features suggested mutual displeasure in the encounter.

"Is there something I can help you with, ma'am?" It paid to be nice. And as this job was the only one paying for someone with her skills—or lack thereof—she'd better grit her teeth. Again.

"I really don't need help today, thank you," Mrs. Hart said, eyes veering away, her manner suggesting what her voice didn't say: "and especially not from the likes of you!"

Mindy simply nodded and tried to look busy as the woman took her time *tsking* at the prices, tutting over the small range of fresh fruit, shaking her head as she pressed the vegetables. Mindy wanted to shake her own head at the sight but protesting the customers' manhandling of produce wouldn't do her any favors, save with her boss, Lionel Bane. And even he was more inclined to keep in the good graces of people like Mrs. Hart than give her a friendly reprimand. Still, when the bruises on fruit appeared, she knew who Mr. Bane would blame. The person on Elnora who never got anything right.

Mrs. Hart finally drew closer, her tiny, wheeled cart crammed high with goods. One of the more interesting aspects of her job—probably the only interesting aspect—was playing "guess what people are having for dinner" from their purchases. Sometimes it was easy: microwave lasagna for one, like poor Mr. Jameson. Other times, like now, it was more of a challenge. Usually she might hazard a guess, in an effort to keep Mr. Bane happy as he wanted her to maintain friendly customer relations. But Mrs. Hart had never been predisposed to friendliness towards Mindy, even before the mess of the last few months. Perhaps it was best to keep quiet and hope this encounter would go more pleasantly than the last.

REGAINING MERCY

Tissues. Flour. Collards. Spices. Mindy scanned and bagged, scanned and bagged. She just needed to keep her eyes down, mind on the job, get this done and get Mrs. Hart out of here.

The quiet of the store, save for the occasional beep, seemed to ratchet up the tension, tightening her stomach better than any ab workout.

"So, have you thought anything more about what I said last time?" Mrs. Hart said, her voice syrupy sweet.

Was this a trick question? Had an hour passed by when she had not cringed over what had been said the last time they had met? What was the correct answer now? "I, er, yes, ma'am." She offered a quick nod. Perhaps being seen to be compliant might encourage Mrs. Hart to not resume her attack.

"Then I hope you'll remember it," Mrs. Hart said with a self-satisfied nod, like she was an olden-day queen bestowing platitudes to the peasants.

Mindy's chest constricted, the inner protest of her days spent constantly bowing and scraping roiling through her heart, her mind. Why couldn't people see it for what it was—a mistake? Why, why, *why* did they have to keep going on about it, bringing up the past like a dog dug up a favored bone? Didn't they think their words seared her? She might as well have "tramp" tattooed across her forehead. Would that make the likes of Mrs. Hart and her fellow church botherers forgive her, and show a bit of the grace they liked to sing about on Sundays? She doubted it. *Still*—she exhaled silently—*just get this customer done and out of here.* Then she could breathe. She'd remember instead—

"I really don't know how you think you can manage that boy on your own," Mrs. Hart said with a sniff. "I feel sorry for him, I really do."

Heat streamed across her chest. How dare she? "Jon has everything he needs," she ground out.

"Everything except a father."

She dragged in a long, deep, unfortunately not-quite-steadying breath, as she clamped her lips closed. She would not respond. Would *not* respond!

The door chimed, admitting another customer. She glanced up, freezing at the sight of Dermott Reilly walking in, his swarthy face lighting in recognition, as he offered her and Mrs. Hart a nod before disappearing to the far end of the store, back to where the drinks fridges were located.

She unwound stiff muscles, refocusing on what needed to be done here and now. Mrs. Hart's groceries. She had no time for muscled men of the gardening variety. She had no time for men ever again!

"Mind on the job, please, missy."

She ground her teeth at the reprimand, sure she'd need to visit a dentist soon. Not that she could afford to. Tomatoes. Fresh beans. Milk. Her movements were fast and jerky. Get out, she silently screamed at Mrs. Hart. Get out!

"Do you mind not squashing my bananas? I find that each time I get my fruit and vegetables home there's at least one with a bruise." She made that *tsk tsk* sound again.

"Perhaps if customers did not feel the need to squeeze every little piece of produce, you'd find fewer bruises on your fruit and vegetables," Mindy muttered.

"I beg your pardon?" Mrs. Hart's faded blue eyes snapped dangerously.

A warning she ignored. "I said," Mindy said in a louder voice, "Perhaps if customers did not go around squeezing the fruit and vegetables all the time then you would end up with less bruising on your produce."

"Well, I never!"

About time she did, Mindy thought, tipping into snark that crowed in juvenile glee at the woman's disconcerted expression.

"Mindy Murray!"

Her head whipped around to see Lionel Bane staring at her,

arms crossed, frown deepening the weathered creases on his face. When had he come in? His glare melded into contrition as he hurried to Mrs. Hart. "Elsie, I'm so sorry for my rude assistant."

What? "Mr. Bane, I—"

"Need to apologize, that's what you need to do. Right now, young lady."

Young lady? Come on. Lionel wasn't her father. But maybe she'd acted like a bit of a brat. She shifted on her heels and faced the irate customer again. "Mrs. Hart, I am sorry."

"So you should be," she said, her eyes and voice glacial. "I am not used to being spoken to in such a way. But I suppose it's to be expected from a girl from the gutter like you."

Mindy's breath suspended, memories slamming spikes of shame through her chest.

"Now, Mrs. Hart," Lionel reddened, shooting Mindy a look that seemed half apology, half plea, "there is no need for that."

"And there is no need for me to shop here, not when I could buy better quality goods elsewhere, and save a pretty penny in the meantime." She turned an irate face to the counter again. "You are a disgrace to your poor grandmama. You always have been, and always will be, I'm afraid."

Fresh hurt swathed her in a crushing embrace. Humiliation was nothing new. And how could she argue with the truth? The heat burning in her heart and in the back of her eyes threatened to spill, so she glanced away, lips tight, shoulders slumped, holding herself still as she stared at the groceries cramming the far wall's shelves.

"Do not expect me to darken these doors again. I will not buy from your store while she remains employed here."

Mindy sensed rather than saw the thin finger pointed in her direction, but refused to move, counting the seconds until Lionel demanded her resignation. Inside, her mind screamed: what would she do? How would she and Jon ever survive? This job's paycheck mightn't be much, but was sure better than nothing. Even putting up with nasty customers like Mrs. Hart was worth putting food on the table. Should she apologize again, make it sound more genuine this time?

She heard Lionel's long sigh, one she'd heard a hundred times before, and internally braced. Here it came.

"And I won't shop here if she doesn't," a deeper voice said. Dermott reappeared from behind Lionel's large frame.

What? Mindy's stare followed him as his gaze flickered between Mrs. Hart, Lionel, and herself. How much had he heard? Her stomach writhed. Oh, why did Dermott always appear at just the wrong time and make her feel so puny and pathetic?

"Young man, this does not concern you," Mrs. Hart blustered.

"I'm sorry that you feel that way, ma'am. But when my friends are being bullied and abused you can't expect me to stand here quietly. Especially not when they are simply doing their jobs."

"But she accused me of squeezing the vegetables!" she complained.

"And did you do that?"

"Of course not!"

Mindy glanced at Lionel to catch him raising a disbelieving brow too.

"Well, I—" Mrs. Hart's fuchsia-lipsticked mouth opened then closed, her gaze flitting between them. "I only did what everyone else does."

"But not everyone else has the nerve to then go and accuse the staff of bruising things, when they are most likely to have done it themselves," Dermott said mildly.

Mrs. Hart drew herself up into spine-stiffened outrage. "I see I am not welcome here."

"Now, Elsie, please do not be hasty—" Lionel began.

"I'm sure Mr. Bane welcomes all customers," Dermott continued, "but does not welcome the bullying of his employees or abuse in any form."

Moisture pricked Mindy's eyes, and she ducked her head. Why was he being so kind? And why was she feeling so fragile, like she wanted to burst into tears? After the things she'd gone through—she should be tougher than this.

"Well!" Mrs. Hart heaved out a noisy huff of air. "I shall just have to collect my groceries and go."

Mindy cleared her throat then said in a low voice, "You, er, first need to pay for them."

"Such a nerve!"

"To pay for your groceries? I'm sure you wouldn't want to be accused of stealing, Mrs. Hart," Dermott said, brows raised and arms crossed.

"You accuse me of being a thief?"

Would the outrage know no bounds? Mindy watched as Dermott shifted to the door, as if to block the exit, while Lionel watched on like a stunned spectator at a Grand Slam tennis match between two heavy-hitters. Which made Mindy what—the hapless ball-girl?

"Fine. Here, then." A couple of twenties were slapped down on the counter.

Mindy checked the amount. "And an extra quarter," she murmured.

"Your prices—this place—is simply abysmal!" Elsie Hart spluttered, slamming a coin on the counter. "I will make sure all of my friends know never to shop here again!"

"You do that, Mrs. Hart. We want to make sure no more bullies come through that door," Dermott said, eyes like stone.

She gave a gasp of indignation and stormed through the door Dermott swung open for her, like the gentleman his sweat-stained workwear said he wasn't.

"Bless her heart," he muttered, his expression such that it

sparked panicked amusement in her chest, which swiftly died when she glanced back at Lionel who was shaking his head.

"Oh, Mindy. I tried. I really did."

"What do you mean?"

He hefted out a sigh that sounded like it came from the soles of his worn boots. "I just can't have you making trouble for the customers."

"But, sir, I didn't. I simply mentioned—"

"Mr. Bane," Dermott interrupted, "I'm afraid it was my words that made things worse."

"Yes, I rather think it was." Lionel shot him a narrow look that didn't exactly scream friendly customer relations, before glancing back at Mindy. Oh no. Here it came. For real this time. "Mindy, I feel real awful 'bout this, but I'm afraid—"

"Oh, Mr. Bane, I'm sorry, I promise it won't happen again."

"But Elsie has a lot of influence in these parts, so it might be best you don't come in for a few weeks."

"But what about Jon?"

"I'm real sorry, but it just ain't working out." Lionel moved to the small employee office and retrieved her bag and water bottle. "Here. I'll call you when I need you. I'll put your pay in your account as usual."

"But sir—" She felt her arm grasped in a strong grip.

"Let's go, Mindy," Dermott said in his no-nonsense elder brother way.

"But this isn't fair! This isn't right! Mr. Bane, please—"

"Just listen to your boyfriend there, that's a good girl."

"He's not my boyfriend," she said, pulling herself free from Dermott's grip, even as she writhed internally at her boss—or was it now former boss?—and his sexist comment. Girl? Mr. Bane's brows rose, compelling her to add, "He's not!"

"Sure, sugar," Dermott said, with annoyingly slow curving of lips, as if he found this grimly amusing.

"Mr. Bane, sir, please, give me another chance. I swear this will never happen again," she called.

"In a few weeks," he said, in his harried manner, not looking her in the eye. "I'll call you."

She felt a sudden rush of stupid tears and knew herself finally beaten.

This job, these men, this reputation she would never live down, it was all too much.

And so she meekly allowed herself to be escorted outside, into fresh air, failure and a financially hopeless future.

Made in the USA
Coppell, TX
26 August 2022